THE MYSTERIOUS JOHN GREY

D0317985

Tom Power

Time is the key to the universe

This key cannot be deciphered by ordinary men

Is it yesterday, today or tomorrow,

Were we here before, are we here now

Will we be here again

Contents

Acknowledgements

Thanks to my wife Hannah for understanding when I disappeared for hours back to 1956 when writing this book.

Thanks to the following, for reading my manuscript and encouraging me to publish. Sandra Mullen, Catherine Fitzpatrick, Mary Fitzgerald, Della Power. Margaret Harney. Warren Power. And thanks to you, the reader for buying it.

Thanks to Darren and Fidelma Power for help with cover

The Valley

It was around three o'clock one Saturday afternoon in April. Mickell Power was walking the high road to the east out of the valley of Knockmurrin. He was on his way to visit his grand uncle, Paddy Casey, whom with relations and friends, young and old, had celebrated his ninety fifth birthday the previous night in Dunphy's pub in the village of Kill.

Paddy was in good health, and enjoyed a few pints and a chat in the local pub. Back in the forties and fifties Paddy was the local blacksmith and worked in his forge at Knockmurrin cross. Mickell liked nothing better than to talk to Paddy about his time in the forge, Paddy was a little forgetful at times, but with encouragement from Mickell he could recall most things, half way up the road he turned around to view the scene in the valley below.

It was a lovely April day the furze and blackthorn blossom looked lovely in the sunshine, he could see the old stone bridge and just to the west of the river, the ruins of the forge where Paddy Casey plied his trade, and just above the forge the house where Mickell lived, and where Paddy Casey lived years ago before he married. The crossroads below him divided the valley into four quarters and reminded him of the cross on a homemade cake. On both sides of the valley excavations were in progress on a few new houses. The road he was now travelling went east to Dunhill, the road to the west to Bonmahon, and the road along the bottom of the valley, went north to the village of Kill, and south to Kilmurrin cove.

Mickell was reminded of a short verse a now departed old friend wrote.

"To the east a hill, to the west a hill, to the north, the village of Kill to the south the sea, and in this vale a home for me."

He knew this old man well he lived at the end of the valley and was known as the local poet, and 'twas often he called to his house, where poetry and books would be the topic of conversation. One day shortly before he passed away he gave to Mickell a copy full of poems, and said look after these, when I depart this valley at least some part of me will remain here.

Mickell treasured the poems and recitations and often at functions such as Paddy Casey's party last night he would recite them. The crossroad divided the valley into four quarters and was also farm boundaries, the northwest farm was Cooney's, two in the southwest Casey's and Cowman's, there were four farms in the southeast, Francis Mooney's, Power's, Murphy's and Kavanagh's, the northeast was Tom Mooney's, and neighbouring them was Manahan's.

So here Mickell Power stood, halfway up the valley, looking down to where he had spent all of his twenty two years, and looking at a potential sight for his new house, now that his carpentry business was booming, and thanks to what someone had named the Celtic tiger, everyone was saying the good times were here to stay. With these thoughts in mind, He put his hand in his back pocket for a chewing gum and instead pulled out a photo of himself that someone had taken at the party in Dunphy's pub, he put the photo back in his pocket, and faced the hill again, on his way to his grand uncle's.

Mickell opened the door that led into Paddy Casey's kitchen, and crossed the hall into the sitting room, Paddy was sitting in a comfortable armchair by a Stanley stove, which gave out great heat and very small consumption of fuel, hello' Paddy, how are you feeling after last night. Ah Mickell how ya, ah sure I'm all right, what did I have only a couple of pints and a few half wan's, put on the kettle there and make me a cup of tay, and put a sweetener in it. Mickell knew that Paddy's sweetener was not sugar, but a drop of whiskey, he made the tea and added the whiskey and took it into Paddy then he sat down.

We had a great night Paddy, good music and plenty of chat. Ah Mickell, you must have been fed up of me, talking of times past. Not at all Paddy I enjoy listening to you talking of the forties and fifties, and your time in the forge. It was that recitation you gave Mickell that set me off. The old Forge! That's the one, God it took me back, will you say it for me again. What now.

When you get to my age all you're sure of is now, sometimes I'm not even sure what day, or year we have, are you going to give that poem or not. Ok Paddy, wait till I go and make a cup of coffee to wet my throat. Mickell went to the kitchen made the coffee, took it back to the sitting room and said now Paddy you want to hear The Old Forge again so here we go

The Old Forge

He stood and looked around him where the old Forge used to be
I walked out to meet him and that old man said to me,
I remember that old Forge in the days of long ago,
from all around they'd gather here and that old fire would glow,
I remember too the Blacksmith, he was big, strong, and tall,
As he hammered on the anvil from his face the sweat would fall,
I still can hear the Horses as they stamped upon the floor,
And all around the old Forge yard stood half a dozen or more.

2

An old bag apron tied around him in the Forge he'd hold the shoe,
One hand upon the bellows, that fire was turning blue,
Then he'd take it to the anvil and hammer out its size,

As he tried it on the horses hoof, you would hear a burning noise,
In from the field a man would come, something broken from a plough,
Do you think that you can mend it I'm waiting for it now,
Then someone with a harrow, and how long will it take,
And a shout from the yard, did you make the iron for the gate.

3

That forge it was a busy place, men would work, laugh and joke
Above the thatch year in year out, would rise the Blacksmith's smoke,
That Forge was more to them than just a place of toil,
It was here they'd meet and share their news of truth and lies,
From here the news would travel if someone had passed away,
Or if a child was born at night, that news was here next day,
It was many a game off football was played outside that door,
As all week long they caught and kicked all last Sunday's score

4

Down the road a common cart came noisily into sight,
Coming to the Forge for a pair of bands, fit secure and tight,
And sometimes in the winter when frost was in the air,
Travelling men would come in and sit, and be dry and warm there,
I had travelled with the old man, back down through the years,
I turned around to talk to him, but he had disappeared,
The old Forge now has fallen briars grow out from the wall,
And did I really see him, that old man so big, strong, and tall.

When Mickell finished, Paddy sat in silence for awhile then said, takes me back. Back, to the good old days Paddy. The good old days, the bad old days, call them what you like Mickell, but whatever kind of days they were, they were our days, and we had to live through them, the same as you have to live through your days.

Back in the forties and fifties, the days of De Valera and Arch Bishop Mc Quaid were stark and harsh, Ireland was a depressing place back then, but we thought we were the bee's knees, a good Catholic country, God's Chosen people, and what ever happened to the rest of the world, we were all going to heaven, but now with hind sight, it's all so different, child sex abuse, cover ups, Magdalene laundries, Industrial schools, we have a person in charge of the Church here and when innocent children confided in him about their abuser all he did was swear them to secrecy, and he is not aware of the seriousness of what he did, and he is not been made aware of it by the Government or the media, ah to hell with them all.

You don't know how lucky ye are today, the freedom ye all have, all of ye educated. back then we were all dominated by the Catholic Church, most of us left school at twelve or thirteen, that was the end of your education, you might get a job on a local farm for awhile, and then it was either England or America and to think we hadn't a good word to say about England, but only for England back then most of us would have starved, you can't beat the bit of education, the Church and State always feared education, with education came questions, and questions when asked often enough, had to be answered, the censorship we had here then, books were banned, films were banned we could only read and watch what Church and State allowed us, our writers had to go into exile to get published and earn a living.

I remember the year Russia invaded Hungary I was working in the Forge, the children coming home from school would call in to pump the bellows and get a bit of heat, I asked them what were they doing in school, one of them said they were praying for the Hungarians and the conversion of Russia, he said their teacher told them that Russia was a heathen place, they were taught in school only what their government allowed, the government choose what books they could read, what films to watch, Russia was a communist country without religion, we were a democratic country, with two much religion, both country's had the same policy's, it was a case of the kettle calling black arse to the pot. When I think of it now those children should have been praying for the conversion of Ireland as well as Russia. It depresses me to think of it.

Pick up the local paper there and read me the notes, I'm too lazy to go look for my glasses.

Mickell picked up the paper and read the notes, nothing exciting in them Paddy, someone has bought a new car, a girl from the village has married a fellow from Dungarvan, they are on honeymoon in Greece, congratulations to another girl on giving birth to a baby girl. And what about her husband Paddy said, did he have any say in the matter. She hasn't got a husband Paddy. God hasn't Ireland changed, and changed for the better, to think an unmarried mother gets congratulated in the local paper, and can proudly push her pram along an Irish road, where's De Valera and Arch Bishop Mc' Quaid now?

Mickell continued to flick through the paper. It says here, that a Charles Arscott, and a native of Waterford has died in a nursing home in Waterford, Paddy sat upright in the chair. What did you say? I said a Mr Charles. I know what you said, I heard you the first time, Charles Arscott, by God, Charles Arscott, I had forgotten all about him and his wife Grace, haven't heard of him since he left the valley, he sold out in nineteen and fifty six.

You mean he was from knockmurrin, he was indeed said Paddy and I'm sure it was in fifty six he sold, because it was predicted in the Summer of that year that Waterford would beat Kilkenny in the fifty nine all Ireland, getting revenge for their defeat in fifty seven. What do you mean predicted, slow down a bit, I'm losing you now Paddy. It's a long story Mickell, it started around April fifty six, Can you stay with me for bit longer I'll tell you. Mickell looked at his watch, it was three forty five, he should be going, but Paddy had aroused his curiosity. O k, Paddy I'll stay a few more minutes. Good said Paddy, pour me another cup of tay and put a good drop of sweetener in it this time, my memory needs oiling.

Charles Arscott and his wife Grace lived on the farm in the north east of the valley, Charles was originally from Waterford City his father owned a thriving business there. Hold on a minute Paddy, you mean Manahan's Farm. That's right, Manahan's bought it in fifty six, Arscott's wife Grace was an only daughter and when her mother died, her father Jim Mahoney took it very badly and started drinking a lot, not locally, mostly in the city, he became good friends with John Arscott, Charles father, Jim Mahony lost all interest in the farm and through neglect and drink the farm was soon in debt.

One day Charles and his father drove Jim home from the city. Charles met Grace for the first time. John Arscott told Jim Mahony the only way to save the farm was to get Grace and Charles married. Grace was only a slip of a girl, she was only eighteen or nineteen, Grace's father and Charles father should have known better, he was a lot older than her. I didn't know her that well but they say she was real down to earth, no airs and graces about her not like some of the farmers daughters back then anyway they were married in fifty five. The Arscott's put a lot of money into the farm, they restocked, and repaired the dwelling house and outhouses, and to everyone's surprise sold the lot in fifty six and left the valley of Knockmurrin.

I'm not sure when they left, but I think it was after the harvest was saved, we were still using the reaper and binder in those years, we all gave them a hand with the harvest that year, why that was, I can't remember right now, the summer of fifty six was a strange year in the valley Mickell, and I don't mean the weather, weather wise it was just an ordinary run of the mill summer. Some strange things happened that year, and the strangest of all was John Grey.

Who was, John Grey, Mickell asked. That's a good question, I didn't know who John Grey was then, and I don't know now, John Grey didn't even know who John Grey was. He walked into the forge one Saturday evening in April, an outsider and a stranger in the valley, he had a bump on the right side of his head, and a trickle of blood ran down his face, he was dressed kind of strange, more the like the way people dress today and he spoke, well different to us.

Was, he a foreigner Paddy. No, no there weren't any foreigners around here back then, the nearest thing to a foreigner at that time was someone who came from the next parish, no he was Irish all right and I'm sure he came from somewhere in Waterford. What do you mean Paddy when you say, he spoke different. He spoke, I don't know, I mean he spoke kind of educated, at that time we had our own way of saying things. We would say fill me a cup of tay, John Grey would say pour me a cup of tea, we might say when swimming, the water is fierce cauld, he would say it's very cold, what I'm trying to say is, he spoke more like the way people speak today. Why didn't he tell you who he was, or where he came from. He had, let me think now, what did the Doctor call it, am, am. Amnesia, Paddy. That's the word, he used to predict things, as the years went on and they came true, I was even more mystified, it was no surprise to a few of us here in the valley when President Kennedy got shot, or when the troubles broke out in the north, the collapse of the twin towers, the Asian tsunami, it was all predicted.

Sometimes when he'd say something we didn't understand, someone might ask, what do you mean, John Grey would gaze across the valley and say it's in my mind, I can see it as clear as I see you, maybe I read it or heard it, something to do with where I came from. He was well read, he would read anything he could lay his hands on books were scarce at that time the good ones were all banned. I think

Grace Arscott use to lend him some, and he had some great recitations and poems, he was a good worker, he spent a while with me in the forge, but worked most of the summer on Arscott's farm.

What did he look like Paddy, was he, big, tall or small. My Memory is not what it used to be, it was a long time ago, I think he looked, a bit like you, I can't remember, I can't think of why he left, but I have no doubt it will come back to me. I think he gave a day with your grandfather above in the quarry, at that time Waterford Co Council were beginning to tar and chips all the roads, once a year a steam engine and mobile stone breaker came to the quarry to crush the stones, extra horse and carts were needed by the Council to haul to and from the breaker, they would hire them from the local farmers, I'm sure it was John Grey Arscott sent that year, your grandfather was the overseer on the Council back then.

I know Paddy, I often heard my father talking about the steam engine and the breaker in the quarry he and his brothers use to hang around there when they were children.

The ringing of the phone interrupted Mickell, stay where you are Paddy I'll get it, hello, it's for me Paddy, it's my Mother, Paddy's fine, alright I'll be down in about twenty minutes. I must go Paddy. Hang on a minute it's just come to me what happened John Grey, this will interest you. I'm sorry Paddy I have to go. Wait a few minutes Mickell. I'd love to Paddy but I can't, Brian Mooney is on his way down to spread a couple of bags of manure on the acre, I'll have to wait until I see you again to hear what happened to the mysterious John Grey, will you be alright. I'll be grand. I'll come up around eight o' clock, we'll go to the village for a pint, John Grey has really aroused my curiosity you can tell it all to me tonight, see you Paddy.

Mickell was walking back down in to the valley, when he heard a tractor in Mooney's field, he knew it was Brian Mooney finishing off his own field and then he would go down to his, he decided to go into the field and get a lift down from Brian, as he was climbing over the fence a loose stone gave way and he fell, head first back on to the road.

The Stranger

It was about four thirty one afternoon in April Paddy Casey was in his Forge a horse shoe held in the fire, one hand pumping the bellows. Paddy took the horseshoe from the fire and brought it to the anvil as he hammered the shoe he noticed a shadow in the doorway. Paddy said "will you come in or go out, it's dark enough in here without blocking the bit of sun light, the man stepped into the Forge. Paddy walked out to the Forge yard to try the shoe on a grey horse then he dipped the shoe into a trough of water that was against the Forge wall, and went back into the Forge. Well said Paddy what can I do for you.

The man stepped closer to Paddy he could see a trickle of blood on his face. What happened Paddy asked, let me have a look. The man had a bump on his head just over his temple, what happened Paddy asked again. I don't know the man answered. What's your name, I don't know that either answered the man. Sit down near the fire there and wait till I put the shoes on the grey, Arscott's man should be calling for her soon, and then I'll take you across to the cottage to meet Kathleen, she will clane you up.

Kathleen was Paddy's sister and they both lived across the road from the Forge. Paddy finished the grey mare, closed the door and tied the mare to a hook on the Forge wall to wait to be collected by Arscott's man. Then Paddy and the stranger went across the road to the cottage, as Paddy entered he shouted Kathleen where are you, I have someone here who's injured have a look at him will ya.

Kathleen came from one of the two small bedrooms that led from the kitchen, another door led to a small annexe about six feet by four, a fire was lighting in an open grate in the kitchen, a hook hung on a bar across the fire. Kathleen said to the man sit here by the fire, she then took a kettle of boiling water that was hanging on the hook and poured it in to an enamel basin, and then went to the annex and came back with a tin box she took a bottle of dettol and a cloth from the box, poured some dettol into the basin, then said to the stranger now come over here and let's have a look at you.

Paddy took the empty kettle, filled it and placed it back on the fire saying, we'll have a cup of tay when you're claned up. Kathleen wiped the blood of the man's face and examined the cut on his forehead, it's not bad she said, just a scratch I'd be more worried about the bump there on your head, Dr. Walsh will be doing his rounds Monday morning, he usually calls in for a dozen eggs, we will ask him to have a look.

As well as the Forge, Paddy had about four acres on which he kept a few calves, a couple of pigs, and a scattering of hens, as Kathleen made the tea, Paddy took another basin and a bar of soap, went to a barrel of rainwater at the side of the house where he washed his face and hands, when finished Paddy went back in, sat at the table and asked the man to join him, you will have a bite to ate with us Paddy said, Kathleen sliced some brown bread, and cold bacon, poured out three cups of tea then refilled the teapot.

They ate in silence, then Paddy said, I asked you before, and now I'll ask you again, where did you come from and what's your name. I don't know the man answered, I can't remember anything I can't even remember my name, I remember standing at the door of the Forge, and everything since, but nothing before that. Christ Paddy said that's strange, but we will have to call you some name, I have an uncle in America called John, you look a bit like him so we'll call you John for now, maybe by tomorrow or Monday you will remember your own name, you can stay in the Forge tonight, I'll put some coal on the fire, give the bellows a pump a few times, it should give you enough heat for the night.

Paddy got up from the table, went to the annexe for a bucket and said to Kathleen I'll go down to the well, the man said I'll come with you the fresh air will do me good. Paddy handed the man one of the bucket's and they crossed the road and over the style to the well, the well consisted of a large concrete pipe standing in the middle of the bog, a hole was cut at the bottom of the pipe on one side where the water flowed in, and another hole at the top at the opposite side where the water flowed out.

Paddy held his bucket under the gushing water then handed it to the man, he took his empty bucket and filled that, Paddy then took out his pipe and tobacco, put one leg on top of the well and lit up. The stranger stood in the middle of the bog looked slowly around him in all directions, trying to figure out where he was, he could see Paddy's Forge about fifty yards to the north of the well and below it a small thatched cottage, they were standing in a valley, he could hear a river flowing just below the well, and a hill to the east, and to the west, he didn't recognise anything. Come on Paddy said, Kathleen will be waiting for the water.

You sit by the fire there Paddy said, I must go up to Arscott's with the grey mare, his man is not coming now I won't be long, Kathleen will get some blankets from the loft, she will fix you a cosy corner in the Forge, I'll get some coal when I get back, who knows with a good night's sleep you might remember who you are in the morning. The stranger was bedded down in a corner of the Forge, he had vigorously pumped the bellows, and the fire gave out a warm glow.

As he lay there he tried hard to figure out the events of the day, but no matter how he tried he could only remember back to when he stood at the Forge door, it was as if only one part of his brain was functioning and the rest was sealed off, as if someone pulled down a shutter, and try as he might he could not lift that shutter to reveal who he was, or where he came from.

The opening of the Forge door woke the stranger. Paddy entered saying are you getting up at all today, Kathleen and I are back from mass and you're still in bed. Mass said the stranger I don't understand. Don't tell me said Paddy that you can't even remember mass. I can't remember nothing the stranger answered, where, am I. You're here in the Forge Paddy answered, you rambled in yesterday evening with a bump on your head, no name and no past. Ah yes the man said I remember now. You remember who you are said Paddy. I don't the stranger said I remember coming in yesterday evening and no more. Ah" well, said Paddy give it a chance it will come back to you, come across to the house, Kathleen will have the kettle boiled, you can use one of my blades to shave yourself, we will be having the dinner soon you can skip the breakfast, by the way Paddy said I'll have to call you some name I said yesterday we would call you John and so we will, and when I first saw you, you were standing next to the grey mare, so I was thinking, what about John Grey. It's as good as any said the stranger. Right then said Paddy John Grey it is.

Paddy and John crossed the road to the cottage, Paddy said Kathleen, meet John Grey. He remembers his name said Kathleen. No Paddy said that's what we are going to call him. John entered the small annexe where Kathleen had poured hot water into the basin. John got Paddy's razor took a blade from a small packet which had Macs Smile written on it, as John looked in the mirror it was as if he was looking at himself for the first time, he didn't recognise his own face, who are you he said, where are you from, what are you doing here. When John was washed and shaved he went back into the kitchen, Paddy was sitting at the fire reading the Sunday paper. Kathleen opened the bottom door of the cupboard and took out a bottle of Power's whiskey and poured a glass for John. I don't know if I should said John I don't know if I drink or not.

Take it as a medicine said Kathleen. Paddy said we have a guest in the house and you expect him to drink alone. Ah" Kathleen said you have no bother remembering whether you drink or not. When dinner was over Kathleen took the dishes from the table, Paddy reached up to turn on the wireless which was on a shelf over the table, then he picked up his paper again and sat by the fire. Some of the lads are calling around at two o' clock John, we are going up the Glen to hunt a few Rabbits you can come with us if you like. I don't think so Paddy, I don't want to go running and jumping over ditches until I hear what the doctor has to say tomorrow. Maybe you're right John. I think so Paddy I might go for a quiet walk down the road.

John was walking down the valley road towards Killmurrin Cove, the sun was shining, the sky was blue, a lovely April afternoon, he heard the Cuckoo in the glen, a small stream flowed from the glen, crossed under the road to join the larger river on its way to the cove. John leaned over an iron gate to listen to the Cuckoo, he then turned and looked up the east hill of the valley, he could see cows and sheep grazing, the furze and blackthorn were in bloom.

John stood there admiring the scene and wondered, how many people had admired that same scene in the past, and how many more would admire it in the future. To the northwest of the valley John could hear men shouting and dogs barking, he knew it was Paddy and his friends hunting rabbits. John continued his walk towards the cove, as he walked he tried hard to remember who he was and where he came from, but he could only remember back to Saturday evening and standing at the Forge door, then suddenly the words of a poem entered his mind. John had no idea where the poem came from, or who wrote it, but in the hope that it might reveal something from his past he started to recite it

A Country Sunday

I walked out this morning the country side to see,
The sun was shining all around it warmed the world and me
The green grass it was growing, and this I'll have you know,
I heard the trout stream laughing, I stopped to watch it flow,
The birds I heard them singing, they were flying all around ,
I saw the cattle grazing, their head bent to the ground,
The rabbits, they were playing, they skipped about the glen,
They stopped to watch as I went by, then hopped and skipped again

2

The sheep were like large mushrooms, white spots against the green,
A kestrel hovered overhead, then dived on something he had seen,
The wild flowers they were blooming, I could see them everywhere
I saw a pheasant flying, a flash of colour through the air,
The hawthorns were in blossom, all through the countryside,
I saw a fox go running, in search of a place to hide,
I watched the sun rise slowly, up in a cloudless sky,
I stood alone with nature, no happier man than I.

Chorus

Through a country Sunday, I slowly made my way
Walking out with nature this lovely sunny day
Blue skies overhead, green grass beneath my feet
And all of God's creatures are there for me to meet

3

The furze upon the hillside, were a brilliant green and gold,
I gazed upon their beauty, and heard their buds unfold,
I sat upon the old bridge, and watched God's work of art,
To be out among this beauty, such gladness filled my heart,
I had shared some time with nature, in those fields around my home,
And I know that I'll return here, no matter where I roam,

For this is where my heart is, and where I want to be,
Just walking along with nature, and all nature's things to see

John finished the poem, fell silent for a few seconds, waiting for something from his past to come to his mind but nothing came.

Monday morning John was woken by loud shouting from the forge yard. Paddy, Paddy, where are you, anyone out of bed around here this morning. Paddy crossing the road answered him. Christ Patsy, be quiet or you'll wake the dead what do you want. Arscott sent me down with this harrow, a few links are broken he's waiting for it now to harrow the high field.

Is he going to harrow it himself or are you doing it Paddy asked. He'll start it, but I have no doubt that I'll have to finish it Patsy answered. All right Patsy give me a chance to get the fire going then we'll see what we can do with that harrow, Paddy opened the Forge door and John Grey walked out.

Who have we here, asked Patsy. John Grey, answered Paddy, he came in yesterday evening a bump on his head, and no idea who he is. And how do you know his name asked Patsy. We don't Paddy said, that's just a name I gave him I let him sleep in the Forge last night the doctor will be calling around soon for some eggs I'll ask him to have a look at him. Paddy said John meet Patsy Hayes. Throw some coal on the fire John, then go across to the cottage, Kathleen will get you something to eat, when the Doctor calls he will have a look at you.

John entered the house, Kathleen had the tea made, and two boiled eggs on the table, sit down she said to John, and get those two eggs into to you, no point in meeting the Doctor on an empty stomach. John buttered some brown bread and poured out a mug of tea, he had just finished eating when he heard a knock on the door, he heard Kathleen say come in Doctor you're welcome. Good morning

Kathleen the Doctor said I've come for my eggs. I hope you don't mind Doctor if I ask you to have a look at someone Kathleen said. Not at all Kathleen that's my job is Paddy sick. God no Doctor he's as healthy as a trout, Kathleen brought the Doctor into the kitchen and said this is John Grey Doctor, he rambled in here yesterday a bump on his head, and he can't remember his name.

Good morning John. Good morning Doctor. Let's have a look at you then, I believe you have no idea who you are, how do you know you're name.

I don't, John Grey is the name Paddy gave me. What happened you. I don't know Doctor, I can't remember anything, and I have a lump on the side of my head, all I can remember is walking into the Forge on Saturday evening everything before that is blank. Let's have a look the Doctor said, not too big, you either got hit by someone or something, or else a fall, have you any headache. No Doctor. Have you double vision. No. Are you sure you can't remember anything before Saturday evening. No Doctor, well maybe, I don't know if it means anything, yesterday when walking down the road, a poem came to my mind.

A poem the Doctor said. Yes a poem, said John. And what is the name of this poem. A Country Sunday, John answered. Never heard of it, said the Doctor. How do you, remember the name. I don't remember it Doctor. I just seem to know. Did you remember all of the poem. Yes doctor, I even recited it, hoping when I finished something else from my past might follow through. And, said the Doctor. No nothing Doctor. Well you have no headache or double vision, so I'll rule out concussion, you're probably suffering from amnesia.

But why the poem Doctor, why did I remember that. You must like poetry, or maybe you were talking about poetry or reciting it before your accident, the part of your mind that's shut off now, will from time to time reveal something from your past, like a poem or a snippet of information, that's a good thing, one of these bits of information will eventually allow your mind to reveal all. How long will that take, Doctor. Who can say, a week, a month, I don't know I'm just a country Doctor, you are quite healthy, so don't worry, my advice to you is to carry on as normal, live for the present and your past will reveal itself when it's ready, now I have to go, thanks for the eggs Kathleen, give my regards to Paddy, if you need me you know where I am.

The Visitor

Two weeks had passed since the visit of the Doctor, John had taken his advice and carried on as normal as he could, he was working in the Forge with Paddy, and sleeping there at night, sometimes when gazing across the valley during the day, in his mind he would see things that he could not explain, visions of very large machinery driving through the fields, strange looking motor cars and large lorry's travelling the roads, in bed at night he could hear people talking, he didn't mention this to anyone he thought the visions could be caused by whatever caused the bump on his head, he was getting on well in the Forge and was good with his hands making things and measurements seemed to come natural to him.

Paddy had a large millstone that lay flat in the forge yard that he used to band the wheels of horse's cart's, he showed John how to place the stock of the wheel into the hole in the centre of the millstone, and how to hammer the bands on to the wheel. One afternoon John was repairing a plough that somebody had brought in from Mooney's, when he saw a man on a horse coming over the bridge. He was about five nine in height, a bit on the heavy side, red face, black hair going bald, John guessed he was in his mid thirties. He turned the horse into the forge yard, dismounted, and handed John the reins saying tie him to the hook on the wall. John took the reins, and the man entered the Forge, John continued working on the plough.

About twenty minutes later the man came out of the Forge, untied his horse, said goodbye to John and rode off. A minute or two later Paddy came out saying that's Charles Arscott, owner of a quarter of this valley, lave what you're doing there John, we'll go up to the house and have some tay, I have something to tell you.

Paddy and John were drinking tea at the table Kathleen was washing spuds for the dinner. Paddy said Charles Arscott was asking about you John.

If Charles Arscott wanted to know something about me, why didn't he ask me, instead of going behind my back. Now take it asy John it's not what you think, he has a vacancy for a handyman on the farm repairing the houses, mending the gates and horse's cart's, he has heard that you are good at that type of work, the man he had went to England last week, he didn't want to take you away from me unless I was willing to let you go, if I wasn't willing to let you go then nothing would be said to you. Does the fact that you are telling me this, mean you are willing to let me go.

We've been busy for the last few weeks John, but that won't last, the Forge won't be busy enough for the two of us, Charles Arscott is offering you a job, and a roof over your head, if you want it, if you don't you can stay working in the Forge as long as the work lasts, but by then Arscott's job will be gone, my advice to you is to take it, the pay is not too bad. I'm sorry Paddy for being a bit hasty, you are right of course, you and Kathleen have been very good to me, I know the work in the Forge is only temporary, I should take the job. I think so John.

When does he want me to start? He was hoping you might call up tomorrow. What's he like Paddy. I don't know much about him John, I don't see him very often, the workmen bring his Horses here, he calls in now and then. He married into that farm, it was Mahony's farm, Mahony had only one child, a daughter, Grace is her name, people say Mahony went broke, and Grace married Arscott to save the farm, some who work in the house say they don't get on, and that they even have separate bedrooms.

By God Paddy John said, that's a bad foundation for a marriage. It may not be true John, people like to let on they know a lot about the people they are working for, it makes them feel important, a lot of it could be just rumour.

Arscotts

It was a fine morning around the middle of May, John Grey was walking up the east road of the hill on his way to Arscott's farm, halfway up he stopped and looked back into the valley, he could see the old stone bridge, and the smoke rising from the forge chimney, on the west side of the valley he could see a man scuffling spuds, somewhere in the distance he could hear a man shouting at cows, on the road below he could see a horse and cart with milk churns on the way to creamery, the birds were singing, the hawthorn blossoms were in bloom. John thought it was a beautiful sight, the words of a poem started to form somewhere in his mind, remembering the words of the Doctor, John started to recite the poem, hoping that in doing so something else in his mind might be unlocked,

Beauty

With gasping breath, and unbelieving eye
He saw the beauty of dawn appear in the sky
Was he dreaming, or was he awake
Such beauty, his heart could not take
But there it was before him laid
The beauty of the world in a quiet glade
Beauty, fire of the heart
with peace cover the earth
Beauty to know you live
Is more joyful than a winters day giving way to spring
Beauty you are there, so wonderful, so brave
Like an elegant yacht, on a crested wave
A precious gem for all to see

Created by nature for you and me
He turn's his head, and looks around
Looks at the sky, looks at the ground
And everywhere he can see
What a wonderful place this world can be.

John continued up the hill and turned in the boreen to Arscott's farm. The boreen divided the field in half, at each side of the boreen cattle and sheep were grazing, and chewing the cud, some were standing, some lying down, rabbits ran towards the ditch as John approached, at the end of the boreen John came to an iron gate which hung on the gable end of a house and was bolted to the gable end of another house, John opened the gate and entered between the two gables into a square farmyard. To his left he could see a large double storey building facing east, John assumed this was the dwelling house, across the yard were more house's, in front of one of the house's, an implement with four legs and on its side a wheel with a handle, leading down to the house was a low cow house, its back facing south for shelter, and to the right were more houses, a stable and a work shed.

John took in this scene, he had never seen a farm yard like this before, or if he had he could not remember, in the middle of the yard was a water trough and pump, a man was standing at the pump, pumping water into the trough. John approached him, John said hello I'm looking for Mr Arscott. How ya the man said, I'm Billy Rourke. Mr Arscott is not here, he had to go to town, you must be John Grey, the new tradesman. Mr Arscott said you would be coming in. The man stopped pumping the water, moved something on the pump, then started pumping again, but no water came, Billy saw the surprised look on John's face, Billy said do you see that tank on the gable end of the dwelling house, that's the water supply for the house I've redirected the water to fill the tank.

Grace Arscott was looking out the window when John entered the yard, she watched as he stood observing the scene, she watched as he walked across to Billy, and she watched as they stood there talking, she knew that Billy would come to the front door and tell her that someone wanted to see her, Charles had told her he would be coming, and that she was to meet him, explain his duties and show him where he was to stay. She had heard the workmen talking about the mysterious John Grey, who had walked into Paddy Casey's Forge one Saturday evening in April, not knowing who he was, or where he came from, they said he could often be heard reciting poetry, she thought it unusual that a workman would be reciting poetry, she wondered who's poetry he was reciting, where he had learned the poems, she thought to herself, I'll have to get to know you John Grey, you really are a mystery. Grace decided to go out to the farmyard before Billy came to the door. John was looking across at the dwelling house, when the door opened and Grace stepped out, he watched her as she came across towards him and Billy, she was tall and slender, shoulder length fair hair, a beautiful face and a slightly tanned complexion as smooth as porcelain, she wore a light green summer dress a bit below her knees, and ankle length boots, as she approached the water trough, Billy said. Mrs Arscott, this is John Grey, he's come about the job.

John said hello. Grace said how are you, my husband said you would be calling he had to go to Waterford to meet his brother. The Priest is it Billy said. Grace looked at Billy and said I'm sure you have enough water pumped Billy. Billy picked up his sprong and went across to the cow house, Grace and John stayed by the pump, Grace said. So you are John Grey. I am John said for now and for the past three weeks, who, or what I was before that, I have no idea. What's it like Grace said not knowing who you are, or where you came from. Strange John answered, some things look familiar, and some things I never saw before, the water pump for instance, that machine across the yard what, is it. A turnip grater Grace answered, it's used for grating down turnips, and mangles for animal fodder. And yet john said, some things look familiar, coming up the hill this morning, I looked back into the valley and I was sure I had stood there before and looked at a similar scene, but was it here or somewhere else, I don't know anyone here in the valley, if I do I can't remember, but if I was from here, the people here would remember me. I'm sure your memory will come back some day Grace said, now come with me and I will show you the workshop.

John walked with Grace to the east side of the farmyard, where she entered an open door, he followed her in, and looked around the room, in the middle of the floor was a timber workbench, hanging on the wall were the various tools of a carpenter, some of the tools looked strange to John, yet he seemed to know what they were all for. Charles said to tell you that the hay shed need repairing, the winter storms have damaged it, some of the other houses and gates also need repairing. Charles said after a few days you will know what to do yourself, Grace moved across towards a stairs in a corner of the room, she climbed the stairs, John followed her.

This is where you will stay she said. John saw a bed and a table, a small round stove, and a cupboard. It will be a big improvement to sleeping in the Forge John said.

I must be going now Grace said, are you going to start work today or must you move your belongings up from Paddy Casey's. I'll start today John said I have nothing much to move. Charles said to tell you that sometimes you must help in the fields at hay time, and at harvest, and on other occasions when the need arises. All right John said. John Grace said is it true that you recite poetry. It's true, John answered, where ever I came from, poetry seems to be all I brought with me, the Doctor said whenever a poem came to my mind to recite it, it might help to connect me with the past. Could you recite one now Grace asked. No John answered. I'm sorry Grace said, it's just that if I heard one of your poems I might know the poet, and what era he came from, it might help you remember.

I'm sorry Mrs Arscott I didn't mean to be rude, it's just that I can't recite a poem on order, they're not always in my mind, and sometimes for no apparent reason and most unexpected, a poem will come to mind. I understand Grace said, I will send Bridget over with a note book and a pen, when a poem enters your mind you can write it down then you can read the poems whenever you want. Thanks John said that would be good. I really must go now Grace said, I, I hope you like it here.

Grace walked back to the house, Bridget Walsh was in the kitchen making tea, Bridget worked for Grace, cooking, cleaning, and any other work that had to be done around a busy farm house. Grace said pour me a cup Bridget please. Yes Mam Bridget said. Bridget how many times have I told you to call me Grace, Mam is stuffy and for older people, God Bridget I'm younger than you. Grace sipped her tea and said to Bridget what do you think of our new man John Grey. I don't know much about him, Bridget answered, only what I hear the workmen say, that he walked into Paddy Casey's one evening not knowing who he is or where he came from, they say he talks to himself a lot. Reciting poetry Bridget, not quite the same as talking to himself. Poetry is it, poetry, that's not going to do him much good around here, Bridget answered it won't mend the barn, save the hay, or cut the corn. All right Bridget Grace said, but you must admit it's rather unusual. Odd I'd call it said Bridget. I don't know said Grace I think he's interesting I'm looking forward to getting to know him.

John had settled in well at Arscott's and had got to know the other workmen, Billy Rourke who he had met at the water trough, and

Patsy Hayes, who he had met below at Paddy Casey's, and a girl named Bridget Walsh, who worked in the house, cooking, cleaning and washing, he had met Bridget for the first time when she brought over the pen and note book from Mrs Arscott, Bridget was a bit on the plump side, about five foot four, ginger hair, she had introduced herself to John saying, I'm Bridget Walsh, Mrs Arscott sent these over to you, so you are John Grey, the new handy man. I am John answered, how handy I am I have yet to find out. Ah you'll be grand here Bridget said, Mrs Arscott's nice and asy to get on with, and I think she likes the ould poetry, Mr Arscott is a bit on the contrary side, but we don't see much of him, spends most of his time in town, anyway I must go back to the house, I'll see you around, at the door Bridget turned around, saying Mrs Arscott seems to have taking a liking to you, sending you over pen and paper and all, see ya.

The Cove

John was in his work shop sawing some timber for the hay barn, as he looked out the window he saw Bridget at the pump washing some milk buckets, he decided to go down and talk to her, as he crossed the yard, he said Bridget any chance of a drink of that lovely fresh water. Plenty of it here Bridget said and it's free, help yourself. John pumped the water with one hand and with the other scooped some into his mouth, saying ah that's good, he then said to Bridget Paddy Casey and I are going up to Kill village tonight, we're going for a few pints, and then down to Baldwin's hall to the dance, would you like to come with us.

I'm going to the dance myself Bridget said, I'll see you all there, but I can't go to the pub with you. Why not, John asked. Young girls don't go into pubs Bridget said. Why not, John asked again. It's just not done said Bridget some of the older married women go into the snug for a glass of stout. What's a snug asked John. God Bridget said do you know anything, a snug is a little small room away from the bar where some women take a drink while waiting for their husbands single women never go there. And why don't they, asked John. Bridget said they just don't, it's not done, public houses are places where young women just don't go, it's frowned on. By whom, asked John. By the men and by the clergy Bridget answered. The day will come John said when there will be just as many women in public houses as men. Never, said Bridget that will never happen. It will, John said, and smoking will be banned in pubs. You're joking Bridget said, what kind of an egit would ban smoking in pubs, who'd go in to them, they might as well close them, any way how do you know asked Bridget. I just know answered John. It seems to me said

Bridget you know more about the future than you know about the present.

John went back to his workshop, shouting across the yard at Bridget I'll see you at the dance tonight, John finished the wood he was cutting, stood it in a corner, then he looked at the clock on the wall, it was one o'clock, as it was Saturday most of the men had a half day, John went upstairs and had a wash and shave, washed his shirt and hung it in front of the fire to dry, then had a bite to eat, washed up, and went down to Paddy Casey's.

Paddy was in the Forge, John entered. Paddy said how, are you getting on above. Great Paddy all the lads are all right, and Bridget is a grand girl, she's going to the dance tonight. Patsy will be delighted Paddy said, I think he has a bit of a graw for her what are you doing for the rest of the day John. Nothing much Paddy, do you want a hand here. No I'm alright, I've got a couple of bands ready for those two wheels there, I'll finish early myself. I think I'll walk to the cove Paddy. Are you going swimming. Gosh Paddy I don't know if I can swim or not. Jump in John and you'll soon find out. I think a paddle will do for now, see you later. Ok John, we'll go to the village early and have a few bottles before the dance.

John was halfway to the cove when he heard a shout behind him, turning around he saw Bridget approaching on a bike. Bridget John said, where are you going. To the cove John, the Arscott's are having a late dinner this evening, Grace gave me a couple of hours off, I must be back at half five. Does that mean you'll miss the dance. No John I'll be up about half ten, since all the men don't come in till the pubs close I'll be plenty of time. When John and Bridget reached the cove, it was very quiet, only three or four people about, Bridget pushed the bike into a small thatched house beside the cove, they walked out to the edge of the tide which was out full, looking to his right John saw a large round hole in the cliff about six feet above sea level, what's out there Bridget.

A small little strand she answered, we call it the back strand. Can we go out there John asked. We can Bridget said the tide is out, we'll go along by the bottom of the cliff, be careful the stones are slippery, Bridget took of the sandals she had on, John removed his shoes and stockings, he followed Bridget as she picked her way along the mossy stones. She was wearing a blue summer dress that ended a couple of inches below her knee. That's a nice dress you have on John said. My sister sent it to me from England. Where in England is your sister. In London I'm going over to join her in September. Why John asked I thought you were happy here. There's no future here for a young girl John, most of the men are old, or married, the young men when they reach nineteen or twenty will go to England or America, no England's the place for me, I'll get a factory job, my own flat, there'll be plenty of young people, plenty places to go, pictures every night, dancing every weekend, not like here, a dance every six months. London's a big change Bridget for someone brought up in the country it can get very lonely there. Ah John, how can you be lonely among thousands of people. You can feel just as much alone in a crowd as in the middle of nowhere, there might be thousands of people there as you say, but you won't know any of them, it's not like here, where you know everyone.

You might have your own flat, or one room in Camden town or Kilburn, but you won't know anyone living above you, or below you, open your front door and walk into the street, all strangers, no hello or how are you, just you alone in a crowd, when you come home from work in the evening and you enter your small room, you are alone until you go to work the following day, that's what happens to a lot of young Irishmen who go there, they can't cope with the loneliness, so they go to the pub, but the pub costs money, but they don't mind, they have friends in the pub, so they go to the pub every night. John was telling this to Bridget as they walked along the base

of the cliff towards the back strand, then a poem he had learned
somewhere entered his mind

Fields So Green

1

I wish I was in those fields so green, where it's peaceful all around
I'd love to be in the country, and leave this great big town
I sit alone in this one small room, I try and save to get back home
But then it gets so lonely here, I go on out and drink some beer
Meet some friends and have a chat, talk of home and going back
And we wish we were in those fields green, where it's peaceful all around
We'd love to be in the country, and leave this great big town

2

But then the months roll into years, and it breaks my heart to be still here
I just can't seem to get away, I drink each night what I earn each day
But I must break drinks cursed grip, and get away and make that trip
It will take me back over the see once more, home again to my native shore
And once again I will be seen, walking through those fields so green
I'll hear the Fox call out his cry, listen to Birds in a summer sky
Walk through a glen at break of day, see a babbling brook go on its way

3

But just right now I need more beer, maybe I'll get home next year
Every day it's getting worse, I can't break this awful curse
Night and day I'm drinking more I'll never see my native shore
I've become a down and out, for scraps of food I search about
Every day I tramp these streets, every night on the ground I sleep
No more I'll see those fields so green, where it's peaceful all around.
No more I'll see the country I'm dying in this old town.

John. John, are you in a dream or something, one minute you are on about loneliness and London then you're gone quiet and saying nothing. Sorry Bridget, I was thinking about something, John didn't mention the poem to Bridget, she was young, she had her dreams, who was he to take them from her, after all some Irishmen and women had become quite successful in England and America, why not Bridget.

Bridget had reached the hole in the cliff that was the entrance to the back strand, it was about seven feet above the beach, Bridget asked for a hand up, John put his hands around her waist and helped her up, she in turn reached down and helped him up, they stood in the middle of the entrance.

John noticed the beach of the back strand was level with the hole in the cliff, the little strand was isolated. To his right, high cliffs and caves, and to his left, a long high stretch of rock isolated the back strand from the main beach, and straight ahead the sea, no house or road could you see, no sign of human habitation. It was like stepping back in time, back to the age of dinosaurs, nothing had changed much here since the dawn of civilisation, what a place John said, what a place, all we need now, is a Pterosaurs to fly overhead. And what kind of a thing would that be Bridget asked. Never mind Bridget, just breathe in deep, breathe in this wondrous wild place, breathe it into your body, into your soul, so it is part of you, and you are part of it, and where ever you are in this world you can close your eyes and picture this place and say, I am off a wild place and it is there I want to be.

Bridget and John ran down the stony beach, along the water edge, in and out of caves, frightening seabirds and a seal that was dozing in the sun, then they collapsed on a small margin of sand that separated the stones from the water and lay there for awhile. Bridget asked John was he going swimming. I don't think so John answered, I have no togs. Neither have I said Bridget, but that's not going to stop me, Bridget lifted her light summer dress over her head and stood there in her knickers and vest, and ran into the water where she ducked, dived, screamed and jumped up and down, then she ran out of the water, shook her hair, jumped up and down on the sand to shake of the water, she picked up her dress went behind a large rock, came back a few minutes later her dress on, and her wet underwear in her hand.

I have to go she said to John, or the Arscott's won't get any dinner this evening. They walked up the beach together, reaching the hole in the cliff, John climbed down, then reached up caught Bridget by the waist and lifted her down, Bridget took her bike from the thatched house John noticed it was a man's bike she had borrowed. Bridget he said you get on the bar and I'll peddle us to Arscotts.

As they peddled towards the Forge Bridget said that was a lovely couple of hours. It was John said but don't tell Patsy I was with you, he'd do me in, he likes you, you know. Ah Patsy's nice, but I'm not going to marry Patsy or anyone else here, I'm off to my sister in England in September. John got off the bike at the gate to Arscot's yard opened it and walked in, he saw Grace standing at the door, saluted her and said to Bridget I'll see you tonight, then went across to his room.

Well Grace said did you enjoy your afternoon off. I did Bridget answered. Where did you go? To the cove Bridget answered holding her wet underwear in her hand. Grace said I see you went swimming. Yes I did. Without a swimsuit Bridget. Well I forget to bring one with me, I didn't realise the day was going to be so good, it was so nice I just had to go for a dip. Did anyone see you Grace asked. We were out the back strand. We, Grace said. John Grey was there, but he didn't go swimming. You'll have to be more careful Bridget some men would be delighted to take advantage of a young girl in her underwear. When you are working here I am responsible for you. Oh no Mam I'm sure John wouldn't even think of that. All right Bridget, but don't do it again, now go and take off that damp dress and we'll start preparing dinner. Grace looked towards the workshop and thought, John Grey who are you, a carpenter, a labourer, a poet, what or who are you.

Grace couldn't understand it, but ever since John Grey walked into her farmyard she wanted to see more of him, she looked out her window more than usual, hoping she would see him in the yard, her husband spending time in the city didn't upset her anymore, in fact it gave her an excuse to talk to John Grey, as she became more reliant on him to run the farm, and right now she wanted to talk to him. She said to Bridget I'll be back in a few minutes then went and selected a book from her well stocked book shelves, and went across the yard and entered the workshop and called out John, John are you up there.

When John came out on the landing Grace was half way up the stairs, she said I hope you don't mind me calling like this. Not at all Mrs Arscott, it's nice to have someone to talk to. Please John call me Grace, Mrs Arscott is so informal. Grace, please come in. I want to give you this book John it's called the poems of John Keats. John was holding in his hand his one good shirt that he had been airing at the stove. What, are you doing, Grace asked. John answered I washed this before I went to the cove I'm giving it an air before putting it on, I'm wearing it to the dance. Grace asked are you taking Bridget to the dance. Paddy, Patsy and I are going up early we are going for a few pints before the dance I think Bridget is going to the dance later.

You were with her at the cove today. I met her on the way there we went out the back strand together, it's some place out there completely cut off from the rest of the world, Bridget is a liberated women she had no problem in going swimming in her underwear.

I'm sure you enjoyed that Grace said. Well it certainly made a change from looking at the seals answered John. Grace said I'm responsible for her while she's working here, I wouldn't want anything to happen to her. Don't worry John said with a smile, she was in good hands. I'm sure she was Grace said, now tell me have you only one good shirt. One shirt and one pair of jeans, and one photo of myself, that's all I had when I came to the valley, Paddy gave me a couple of old working trouser's, and the workman that was here before me left an old pair of overalls hanging in the work shop.

We will have to get you some new clothes, Bridget and I are going to Kilmacthomas on Monday, there's a good shop there, Lennon's, a couple of shirts, trousers, and a pullover. Hold on a minute John said I can't afford all those. Nonsense Grace said, I can withhold a few shillings a week from your wages, now what's your size. John looked at the collar of his shirt, seventeen he said. And your waist Grace said. I don't know John answered, I have a measuring tape in the workshop I'll get it, John ran down the stairs and back up with the tape.

He handed it to Grace. Grace looked surprised," me," measure you she said, I, I can't do that. Why not, John asked. But, but grace said. Come on John said it's easy you just but the tape around my waist. I know how to measure someone Grace said.

She laid the book on the table and saw the photo of John she picked it up, that's most unusual John. I'm an unusual kind of guy. I mean the photo it's, coloured. What's unusual about that, John asked. I never saw a coloured photo before. John took the photo from Grace and put it in the press saying are you going to measure me or not. Grace slowly approached John, put one hand around his waist, then the other, she was really close, then she stepped back quickly saying, there now it's done. But John said what about the leg, you will have to measure my leg, OH " Grace said I can't. Well I can't do it myself

John said.

Grace hesitated then she saw John's jeans on the bed, went over and picked them up, and said I can see the waist measurement here, stretched them out on the bed and measured the leg. Sorry John said I forgot about them. I'm sure you did Grace said then picked up the book from the table and handed it to John, I suppose you haven't any books. Not in my present existence John answered, maybe in a previous one.

What do you mean in, a previous one. Before I came to this valley maybe I had books then, who knows, what I had, or what I was, a carpenter, bricklayer, stone mason, teacher, travelling minstrel and poet, serenading young ladies in the hope of stealing a kiss. I hope you didn't try to steal a kiss from Bridget today. What John said and answer to Patsy. Do you think Bridget and Patsy will get together Grace asked. Patsy would like to, John answered Bridget has other plans. True love seldom runs smooth Grace said. I think true love will always run smooth Grace, it's when true love don't exist that's when problems occur, very few marriages are made in heaven, most of them are made by the match maker, marriages of convenience, money, land, anything but love, two people shackled together in misery until death releases them.

God Grace said you make it sound like hell. It could be Grace tied forever to someone you don't love. Were you ever in love John. I don't know Grace. I can't remember, maybe I was, maybe I am, and you Grace, are you in love. I'm a married woman. That's not what I asked, are you in love. Grace hesitated and then said, I, I don't know, I think I am, I must be going now. John said Charles your husband. What about him. I haven't seen much of him around since I started here. Oh he's not too fond of farm work, he's been helping his father in the shop, himself and his brother Fr Richard are coming out this evening, we're having dinner, I must be going now enjoy the dance

I'll see you tomorrow. I hope so John said, John went out on the landing and watched Grace go down the stairs, Grace Arscott he said to himself I didn't try to steal a kiss from Bridget today, but I was very, very tempted to steal one from you when you were measuring me.

Grace crossed the yard and joined Bridget in the kitchen. Are you all right Bridget asked, you look a bit excited. I'm grand Bridget, I think I'll go and get changed now. Grace went upstairs to her room and sat on the edge of her bed, she was feeling a bit confused after the conversation with John, she had John's words in her mind, two people shackled together in misery until death releases them, she wondered did John know that her marriage was a marriage of convenience, why had he asked her was she in love, why had she said she thought she was. She had never been in love she certainly was not in love with Charles, would she recognise love, and when she was measuring John, being so close, such a strange feeling. Grace, Grace, Bridget shouted Charles and Fr Richard are here. Grace was brought back to reality by Bridget's voice. I'll be down in five minute Bridget pour them a drink.

The Village

It was a lovely June evening, Paddy Casey, John, and Patsy Hayes were on their way to the village of Kill for a few drinks, and the dance, they cycled to the bottom of the Manacaun hill, dismounted and walked up, at the top of the hill was the Council Quarry. Patsy said the breaker has moved in. The what, John said. The stone breaker John, it comes here every year to break the stones for the roads, Arscott will send a horse and cart here on Monday.

Why John asked. To haul the stones up to the breaker Paddy answered, we'll go in for a look. They placed their bikes against the ditch and climbed over the gate into the Quarry. John saw a large machine up against a large mound of stones and clay that formed a steep incline that was level with a platform on the machine. What in the name of God is that asked John. It's a stone breaker answered Paddy did you ever see one before. I don't think so said John. The rocks are drawn up the incline and dumped on to the platform near the jaws of the breaker, then the men push the stones into the jaws and they are broken into chips and dust, the chips will be stored here, and then Waterford Co Council will use them to tar and chip all the roads around here, all those dust and gravel roads will be a thing of the past.

But what works it asked John. That Steam Engine over there Patsy said. John looked over and saw a very large machine standing on four iron wheels, and another large wheel attached to its side. Paddy said a belt will be placed around the wheel on the side of the Steam Engine and on to the wheel on the stone breaker, and when the Steam Engine is started the wheel will revolve and the belt will turn the wheel on the breaker and both machines will work as one.

Then Johns saw what looked to him like a timber shed on iron wheels. What's that, John asked. That's a Council van John, the man in charge of the steam engine lives in that Paddy answered, and when he moves on from here to another Quarry that will go with him. The original mobile home John said. Come on Patsy said, it's thirsty work talking about work. The three of them climbed out over the gate and continued their journey to the Village.

They cycled past the Chapel, over the street which had a row of double storey houses at the left hand side, a long single storey pub at the other side which had the name Cooney's over the door, a bit beyond the pub was some waste ground and a small house with a stove pipe protruding through the wall, next to that a cow shed and then a house that was both double and single story, the single half was thatched and double half was slated, the street ended at a cross roads.

The lads dismounted the bikes, Paddy and Patsy saluted some men on the corner. John stood and looked around taking in the scene. The village of Kill consisted of the street they had travelled over, one road to the east which was known as the Waterford road, another pub and shop was on this road, the shop had a couple of bicycles on display in the window, it had the name Baldwin's over the door, a bit below the pub was what John guessed was a hall, across the road from the hall was the School, beside the school a cottage, across from Baldwin's pub was a thatched pub and another shop, the name Sullivan's over the door, on the road west out of the village was the post office and shop, J, J Walsh in neat letters over the door.

Below the post office was a row of two storey buildings and below them two small felt covered house's and across the road from the post office was another pub, this was also a two storey building, with a single storey thatched annex attached to it, the name Fadden's over the door, this pub, as did the other three had written under their name, licence to sell beer, wine, spirits, and tobacco. The only building on the road north was the Garda Barracks, John observed all this in a couple of minutes and thought to himself, there's no shortage of pubs or shops here, he then asked Paddy, which pub are we going to. Paddy answered Sullivan's, we can put our bikes in the shed at the back they'll be safe there.

Paddy, Patsy and John entered the pub through a small porch at the front which led into a hallway to the right was a small shop, a door to the left led into the bar. John thought the pub was dark compared to the bright evening outside, the counter and walls had brown panelling. Paddy and Patsy saluted some of the customers, they all knew each other well, most of the customers were standing at the counter, a few were sitting down, a man sat in the corner near the fireplace with an accordion on his lap.

Paddy called for two large bottles of stout and asked John what he was having. John asked the barman for a pint of Carlsberg. A pint of what asked the barman. Carlsberg said John. What's that asked the barman. It's a lager John answered. Never heard of it said the barman. John said it's a good drink. The barman said it could probably be the best drink in the world but I never heard of it. Ah said Paddy give him a bottle of stout the same as the rest of us. John took a sip from his drink and looked around the pub.

A tall man wearing a hat and smoking a pipe was at the far end of the counter, talking to two other men. Paddy saw John looking and said, the man smoking the pipe, that's Michael Power, he's the council overseer. John said he looks a bit familiar to me. Paddy said he is with Andy Kirwan and Patie Torpey. John said apart from you and Patsy, these men are all strangers to me, maybe if my memory came back I might know them all. John was listening to the talk it was about the weather, haymaking, and Waterford's chance in the hurling. Paddy and Patsy said that Waterford would win the all

Ireland. John disagreed, said they wouldn't win it till fifty nine. Patsy said are you telling me that this is not our year. I am John said, we will win it in fifty nine. How in the name of God can you say that, can you, predict the future.

No, I don't think so it's just sometimes I get these strange visions, maybe they have something to do with my past, or where I came from. Sometimes at night I hear voices, it's as if they come into my room and sit around the bed, they talk about various things to each other and I think they talk to me as well, I just can't understand it. The other day for instance when you were going out the lane with the horses and seed sower, I was watching, suddenly the horses and seed sower were gone and in their place was a huge four wheel machine and another machine attached to the back of it, whether that machine was something from my past or where I came from, your guess is as good as mine, when I went to bed the other night I could hear these voices, they were talking about the hurling All Ireland, someone said we will win it this year, another said we won't, then a voice said it's hard to believe we have only two All Irelands, forty eight and fifty nine. Someone else said we should never have lost the fifty seven final.

I can't explain it, why these things are in my mind I just don't know. Paddy said the strange machines could be from your past, or where you came from but the fifty nine all Ireland is in the future, your past couldn't be the future could it. Past, present, or future, I still say Waterford will win it in fifty nine. A man standing next to John said you make that statement as if you are sure of it. As sure as I can be, John said.

The man introduced himself I'm Taigh O'Brien, the teacher here in kill. I'm John Grey. I've heard of you, you're below at the Forge with Paddy Casey. I was John said, I'm up at Arscott's now. I know Mrs Arscott, Taigh answered, a lovely woman I'm not familiar with her husband though, a kind of absentee landlord I believe. I wouldn't say landlord, absentee yes, I'm there a few weeks now and I've hardly seen him, and yes I do agree with you, Mrs Arscott is a lovely woman. I believe Taigh said you can't remember who you are, or where you came from. That's true answered John, but I'm sure it will come back to me. When you said Waterford will win in fifty nine, how can you be so sure. How can you be, so sure John of something that's going to happen in the future. You heard me talking about my visions, well I believe in them, anyway the past, the present, the future maybe they are all happening at the one time. You mean a parallel universe said Taigh. No said John I mean the same universe.

Paddy said what in God's name are you two talking about, I couldn't be listening to you I'm going to talk to Michael Power and Patie Torpey. Patsy had sat down near the box player. Taigh said John what do you mean, the same universe. John asked did you ever hear anyone say.

Time is the key to the universe
This key cannot be deciphered by ordinary men
Is it yesterday, today, or tomorrow
Were we here before, are we here now
Will we be here again.

I never heard that Taigh answered that's deep. John said let's say some one invented a time machine, and they travelled back to this time last week, what would they find. I suppose they would find the people that were here enjoying themselves answered Taigh. If that is so said John that would prove that last week and this week are existing at the same time, now let's set that machine a week into the future, and we find there, people also going about their business, that would prove that past, present, and future exist at the same time. Taigh said but when they went back if they found nothing, just a void, and the same in the future, wouldn't that prove that it's only the present exist.

Not really John answered, we know for certain that people were here last week, and we know if we could go back we would meet them, we know we are here now, and unless the world is going to come to an abrupt end, people will be here next week, which brings me back to my original statement, the past, present and future, are they existing at the same time.

Taigh said I guess we will never know, unless someone invents a time machine, or solve the mystery of time. And time is a mystery John said, it treats us like a cat treats a mouse, time plays with us, strings us along, and when it tires of us, it disposes of us without remorse. John and Taigh were interrupted by the barman calling silence for a song.

John listened to a man called Tommy O' Brien singing a song called the lonely woods of Upton, then the accordion player played a few tunes, when he finished he asked someone called Nailer Casey to sing the Rose of Tralee which he did, a man named Martin sang south of the border.

Taigh said I'm going to ask John here to give us a recitation I hear he's quite good. The men in the bar shouted encouragement. All right John said, wait till I get Paddy and Patsy a drink, will you have one Taigh. No thanks John. The barman served the drinks. Then John said, I'm going to recite a poem called, Returning, it came to my mind the other day and I wrote it into the notebook that Grace, I mean Mrs Arscott gave me.

Returning

1

Down the road he walked, and there just around the bend
Stood an ivy covered ruin, that was his journey's end
Some thousands of miles he travelled, for something seemed to call
The voices of his ancestors, born within those old clay walls
As he stood outside that place, now empty and decayed
He looks around at quiet fields, where his forebears worked and played
From dawn to fall of night, so hard they had to toil
For their food upon the table, they depended on the soil
Then there came a year when the potato crop did fail
From Valley and from Mountain came an agonising wail

2

The spectre of starvation, cast its shadow across the land
Thousand's died from hunger, while others lived so grand
Evicted and burned out, cast on to the side of the road
Families torn asunder, dying in the wet and cold
Ragged covered walking bones, not dead yet not alive
Scavenging the countryside, desperate to survive
Ireland turned to America in those grief filled years
You threw her out a lifeboat, when she was swamped in tears
Our hard working sons and daughters found refuge on your shore
You gave to them a welcome you never closed your door

3

They sailed across the Atlantic from hunger and from strife
In our darkest hour you were a guiding light
A real good friend and neighbour, you helped them through the pain
You gave a home and work, restored their pride again
And they returned their gratitude, in sweat, tears, and blood
They helped to build your railroad, across mountain plain and flood

They joined your armed forces, fought for the stars and stripes
And when you lost John Kennedy, they cried with you that night
You took in our emigrants, they proved loyal and true
You gave to them a home, and they gave back to you

4

Distinguished sons and daughters, who worked with heart and hand
Descendants of those emigrants, became Presidents of your land
And now some are returning to their forebear's native soil
But not in rags and poverty, they return in style
And a land that once barren is now bountiful again
But the famine is not forgotten here, or the poverty and pain
And as you walk among us, and trod your forebears sod
We will all remember those who died in field and bog
America we will remember, it was you who gave the call
And said come on I'll help you, there's plenty here for all

A loud shout went round the bar when John finished, the accordion player played a few more tunes then said he had to go to Baldwin's hall to join the band. Tommy O' Brien sang another song called my little grey home in the west.

Taigh said to John I never heard that poem before, where did you get it. I don't know John said, I can't remember anything from my past, and yet I can remember these poems, where they came from, or who wrote them, I have no idea. The one you gave now, you mention a John Kennedy who was he. I'm not sure, maybe he was President of America the poem is all about the Irish in America.

No Taigh said there never was an American President called Kennedy, there is a very strong political family in Boston called Kennedy and one of them is called John, he's a senator, but it can't be him, the Kennedy in your poem is dead, this one is still alive. Unless

John said the Kennedy the poem mentions, becomes President in the future. If he did Taigh answered, how could the writer know. Paddy and Patsy came over to John and Taigh come on John Patsy said we better go down to the dance it's not fair to keep them women waiting any longer. John said alright lads I'm coming, then he said to Taigh I have to go. We'll talk again some time to see if we can solve the mystery of time, and those two Kennedy's, or is it one.

The Picnic

Sunday morning John was out of bed at nine o'clock, he made some tea, boiled two eggs and made toast, they had a great time at the dance, with the jigs, reels and sets they drove the dust to the ceiling, John danced with Bridget a few times, and with a good few other women who were all strangers to him, when the dance was over they all cycled and sang their way home. John had intended to go to eleven o' clock mass, but he started to read the book that Grace had brought into him, it was the complete poems of John Keats.

He was so absorbed in the book, he completely forgot the time. It was hearing voices in the yard that disturbed him from the book, he looked at the clock it was twelve thirty John looked out the window. Sitting in front of the hall door was Grace, Charles, and a Priest who John assumed was Charles brother. John got up to put the kettle on but the water bucket was empty. He took the bucket and went down to the pump in the yard.

Good afternoon John Grace said, it's a lovely day. John said hello and began to fill the kettle. Grace then said, come over and join us, I want to introduce you to Father Richard. John went over.

Charles was drinking a whiskey as was the Priest. Grace was drinking tea, will you have something she asked John. No thanks John answered I must go and make myself some dinner. This is Father Richard, Charles's brother Grace said. Glad to meet you John answered. This is John Grey our carpenter. John shook hands with the Priest, who was red faced and rather round. I didn't see you at mass this morning the Priest said.

No I forgot John answered I forgot. Forgot, forgot' said the Priest, how can one forget to go to mass. I was reading, and when I'm reading I'm in another world. What, time did you get home from the dance, Charles asked. About twelve thirty John answered. That's why you didn't go to mass Father Richard said, out all night drinking and the devil knows what, and you can't get up for mass. I was up at eight Father, John said. Did Bridget come home with you, Grace asked. With me Paddy and Patsy, we all cycled home together. Disgraceful said the Priest a women out all hours of the night down a dark road with three men, a chance for the devil to work his wicked ways. Nothing happened, Father.

Nothing happened, nothing happened, where men and women are concerned something always happens Fr Richard said, the devil avails of every opportunity to work his wicked ways and he is very successful with sins of the flesh. They weren't any sins of the flesh Father or any other kind of sins, no sins at all, unless you consider cycling a bike down a country road and singing a few songs sinful.

The trouble with people like you Father, you see evil in everything, you always look for the worse in people. We have to be always on our guard there are enemies of the Catholic Church everywhere, do you believe in a Catholic God. Not really John answered. The Priest banged his glass on the table, how dare you question the one true faith, what kind of heathen are you. I am not a heathen John answered, I am a Christian, I believe in a Christian God, one god for all. Blasphemy said the Priest, whose red face was now even redder, there is only one true church and the leader of that church is in Rome.

There are several churches Father and one God in charge of them all. The Priest turned to Charles and said what kind of heretic have you hired here, he is preaching about other gods, he don't go to mass, he will be a bad influence on the good Catholics of this parish you will have to get rid of him.

Now Richard, Charles said he is a very good carpenter, and either his dancing or his believes don't interfere with his work, how he spends his Sunday is his own business. Grace interrupted. What do you mean John, one God, several faiths. Nonsense said the Priest, utter nonsense, there is only one faith and this man should not be allowed to talk like that

I'll talk anyway I like John answered, do you honestly believe that millions, and millions of people are going to be dammed because they don't believe in a Catholic Church. If they believe in God, whether that God be Protestant, Jewish, Muslim, Buddhist or whatever, as long as they believe they will be saved, do you see that large tree over there, well the trunk of that tree is like God, and all the branches represent different religions, but every branch in that tree is connected to the one trunk, the same as every branch of religion is connected to the one God. The Priest was flabbergasted and was about to answer John when Grace said, I'm sure Bridget have the dinner ready by now let's go inside. John picked up his kettle, I must go I have to make my own dinner, I haven't the luxury of a servant to make it for me, but Jesus Christ had no servant either, he was just a carpenter like me.

John was washing up after his dinner when he heard a car start in the yard, he looked out the window just in time to see Charles and the Priest leave, he picked up his book again and continued to read, after some time had elapsed he was interrupted by a knock on the door, John and Patsy had arranged to go to Kilmurrin for a swim, so he said come in Patsy, a ray of light was shining through the window and lit up the doorway, dust from the timber floor circulated in the sunshine creating a bluish haze, John was expecting Patsy to enter. But it was Grace who emerged from the bluish haze. John stood looking at Grace, speechless for a few seconds, he thought my God she is like an Angel in a celestial beam of light.

Grace said I hope I'm not disturbing you. No, no, not at all John said, I was expecting Patsy. I came up to ask a favour, I know it's your day of, but it's such a lovely day, and Charles has taken the car to drive Fr Richard to town, would you please tackle the pony and trap for me I want to go to Annestown for a swim. I still have a job then said John. Of course you have Grace said, if you still want it. Work is hard to find Grace, of course I want it.

I thought you may not want to work for someone with a servant to cook dinner, I want you to know, I treat Bridget as a friend not a servant, and if she didn't work here she would have to emigrate.

I'm sorry Grace I wasn't referring to you, I know you treat Bridget well, and the work men. It was Fr Richard and the Church I was talking about, they do not walk the road that Jesus walked or preach what he preached, they have no time for the poor of this world, they are only interested in money the church is more like a royal family now with its pomp and pomposity, elaborate dress, ceremonies, Bishop's Palaces, his Grace, his Lordship, Mother superior, and all that nonsense.

How did it come to this from an ordinary man in sandals, who gathered around him ordinary work men, they Church is now like one of those banana third world countries, their leaders driving around like an over dressed Peacock, while eighty per cent of their followers are in rags and poverty, Jesus message of equality for all is well forgotten, even the Pope is now deemed infallible, no longer content to represent God on Earth, he wants to be God, if Jesus came back to day they would probably crucify him all over again.

Listen John if you are heard saying those things you will be ran out of the parish and excommunicated from the Church, Fr Richard takes his religion seriously, not so Charles, I told them at dinner that good trades men are hard to get and that you are quite capable of doing all the other work that is required on a farm, Charles will convince Fr Richard that it's better to keep you.

John said thanks for that vote of confidence, it is a pleasure to be your servant and to tackle the pony and trap for you, and convey you to where ever you want to go. Grace smiled and said I will go and prepare a picnic basket while you are tackling the horse. John had the pony and trap ready in a little over ten minutes.

Grace came out and put the picnic basket on the floor of the trap. John helped her in and handed her the reins. John she said, will you drive the pony is a bit on the giddy side. Your wish is my command John answered.

My wish is to drive down to Dunhill Castle, along the valley road to Annestown, then on to Boatstrand and up to Kilmurrin, a beautiful scenic route on an ideal Sunday afternoon. John thought to himself and a beautiful woman by my side.

The pony trotted along at a brisk pace, Grace was in a talkative mood. You don't know anything about the valley do you john. Only what people tell me John answered. And what do they tell you. Oh that it's a nice place to live, the people are friendly, work is scarce, and a lot of people emigrate. Grace said I'm sure they have something to say about Charles and I. You know what people are like Grace they like to gossip, it's in their nature, if they weren't talking about you they would be talking about someone else. They do talk then Grace said. Yes Grace about you, about me, about anything and everything John answered.

John I know what they say and I can understand, it must seem strange to them the way Charles and I live, me here on the farm mostly on my own, he spending a lot of time in the city, not a good way to start married life. Grace more or less knew what the people were saying about her and couldn't care less, what she really wanted to know was if John knew.

John stopped the pony and said people like to talk and be first with some news it makes them feel important, and stories get added to as they make the rounds, you must have heard the old saying, there are two sides to every story, but I think they are three, you have the versions of the two people involved, and somewhere in the middle the truth. Grace said, tell me what stories you heard and I will tell you if they are true. Well Grace for what it's worth, they say your marriage was arranged to save the farm, that your father got into debt, they say you and Charles have separate bedrooms, that you don't love him, that his father made him give up some woman in the city, that he drinks a lot and can be violent. But when they talk they are not malicious, more concerned about you, it seems the people of this valley have respect for you and your family, they say ye have always treated them fairly, an honest day's pay for an honest day's work.

Grace was silent for awhile when John finished. John flicked the reins and the pony moved on.

Then Grace said with a lot of emotion in her voice, my father always loved it here, this was the only life he knew, when mother died he was completely lost he just couldn't cope, he neglected the farm, he started to drink a lot, not local but in the city, that's where he met Charles father, we were soon in serious debt, the bank was going to sell the farm, one day father came home from town and said I am very, very sorry for what's happened to the farm, but there is a way we can save it, but I want you to know the choice is entirely yours.

Grace John said you don't have to tell me this. I do Grace answered, you are the one person in this world I want to tell it to, I made a mistake John, and when I saw you for the first time that's when I realised what a dreadful mistake I made, all I ever thought about was saving the farm, and when father said that day that Charles's father would pay of the debt if I married Charles, I agreed. Father then signed the farm over to Charles father and me, we married a month later, four months after our marriage Father took ill and died, when I agreed to marry Charles I thought I could grow to love him and make it work, but what happened on our wedding night ended all hope of that.

He got so drunk he could barely stand up or talk, I had to get help to bring him up to our room, then he started on about gaining a farm and losing the love of his life, he grabbed me and threw me on the bed saying let's see how you compare to her, I pushed him off but he grabbed me again, we struggled, I tried to get free, he struck me twice across the face, I kicked him in the, well you know, where it hurts he fell on his knees, I ran out of the room, that was our wedding night, and you are the only person I ever told, he apologised the morning after of course, but we both knew our marriage was doomed. John stopped the pony again and said Grace why are you still with that man. That man's father, own half my farm John, what can I do walk away and leave it all to him. And what about Father Richard does he know the situation John asked. Father Richard played a part in arranging the match between Charles and me and like all arranged marriages he thinks it takes time for them to work, Grace looked so sad and helpless when she finished telling her story. John said you look like you could do with a big hug, would you sack me if I hugged you. No Grace said but I will if you don't.

They were now approaching Dunhill Castle. Tie the pony to the gate John Grace said and let's go up, they climbed the steep hill and into to the ruins of the Castle, John climbed to the highest point of the ruins and stood there looking across the valley, below him the river Anne meandered it's way to the sea at Annestown, he could see the turf bog and the scars left by the turf cutters, here and there in the valley he could see cows grazing, he counted five swans on the river, it was a beautiful place, he went back down to where Grace was sitting on a large stone, what a wonderful place he said to her. But surely John you have been up here before. If I have I can't remember, but I can sense something familiar about this place, he gazed silently across the valley, out to sea, to the horizon and beyond trying to reach into his past, he began to recite a poem.

Dunhill Castle

1

Now empty and forlorn you watch the seasons come and go
But what care you for summer sun or a fall of winter snow
The Ivy now grows green around your ancient wall
No music now or song from within your banquet hall
No noise around you now but the lowing of the cattle
But if I stand and listen I might hear the sound of battle

2

Cromwell came and did lay siege, he attacked and attacked again
But each attack was bravely met buy your mistress and her men
Around your grounds and ramparts the sound of sword and gun
After many days of battle they had Cromwell on the run
But then disaster struck and all because of a drink
No not the alcoholic kind but a jug of buttermilk

3

The chief gunner was dissatisfied, he expected a stronger brew
So above your battered walls the surrender flag he flew
Cromwell did gain entry, revenge was in his eyes
He then blew up the Castle and your mistress bravely died
From inside your broken walls smoke curled up to the sky
But no one loves a traitor, so Cromwell hung the gunner high

4

Now a ruin, you gaze across that lonely Annestown bog
Where you watched them cut the turf, in summers now long gone
You tower above the winding road, a reminder of the past
Below you now on that same road, cars and tractors travel fast
But you go back for centuries, perhaps you can recall
When they were no road, just a path through oak trees big and tall

5

In this peaceful valley now the song birds sweetly sing
The river Anne flow gently by the ruined Castle of Dunhill
And if you pass this way, going to Annestown or Tramore
As you gaze up at the Castle, you might see the mistress De La Poer
Is that her wandering there, where she fought and died so proud
Or perhaps it's just a trick of light, the shadow of a passing cloud.

Grace said that's the history of the castle, you've just told the history of this place in verse, you must have been here before, how else would you know its history. If I was here before I can't remember Grace, who the hell am I, where have I come from, Where am I going. Don't worry John, don't worry, it will eventually come back to you, come on let's go back down and continue on to Annestown.

Grace and John raced down the deep slope, John untied the pony and helped Grace into the trap, Grace untied a ribbon she was wearing around her hair and let it hang loose on her shoulders, she stood up in the trap, John encouraged the horse into a vigorous trot, and with Grace's hair blowing in a mild summer breeze they sped along the valley road and soon reached Annestown bay, although it was a sunny Sunday, they weren't many people around, a few motor cars and a few ponies and traps.

John brought the pony to a halt at the old lime kiln and tied him to a ring protruding from the wall.

Grace stepped down from the trap, and asked John to bring the picnic basket, she took a rug from the seat, folded it under her arm, picked up her bag from the floor of the trap and they both walked across the stones on to the sandy beach, Grace spread the rug on the sand and they both sat down, she reached in to her bag and took out her swim suit and towel, reached into the bag again and took out a man's togs threw it to John saying, I guessed you wouldn't have one with you, that one belongs to Charles, it won't be a proper fit, but what it lacks in length it will make up for in width.

They both lay on the beach silently soaking in the sun, then jumping up Grace said I'll race you to the water, John caught up with Grace just as she reached the water edge, picked her up and continued his run, then with Grace in his arms he dived head first into a large wave, Grace came up spluttering and shouting, wiping the water from her eyes and face, she eventually got her bearings, saw John and jumped on his back knocking him into the water, they then splashed water at each other, and after several minutes frolicking things quietened down.

Come on John said let's swim out a bit, both of them glided easily through the water out beyond the entrance to the bay, then floated on their backs for some minutes, and eventually swam back to shore. Grace said you're a very strong swimmer John you are definitely from the coast.

Then she dried and dressed herself, John let the sun dry him. Grace opened the picnic basket, took out some ham and tomato sandwiches, a bottle of red wine and two glasses. John said so this is how the rich people live. It's just a few sandwiches and a bottle of wine Bridget and I made up, anyway if I was rich I'd have my farm bought back by now, she likes you, you know.

Who likes me John asked. Bridget, Grace answered. And I like Bridget, she is a lovely girl John said, she will make some man very happy, someone who can give her security, a future, what have I to offer anyone, I don't even know who I am, for all I know I could have a girlfriend, maybe I'm married, any woman who is looking for a husband, a home, and a tomorrow should stay well away from me. Grace said and what about a girl who already has a husband and a home, should she stay well away from you as well.

Depends on who that woman is John said, if she is the beautiful woman who has just told me her problems, and is now lying on a beach beside me, and whom I think I'm in love with since the first time I saw her, and I want to desperately take in my arms and kiss, but I'm afraid to do so because she might take offence. Before John could say anymore Grace said John don't, don't I'm a married woman.

In name only John said. Grace said, John I'm so confused, I want so much to be with you but I'm married, you could be married, you don't even know who you are, what future can we have, as I said I'm married, maybe in name only, but here in catholic Ireland marriage is forever, it's madness, what hope have we.

The hope that comes with love John said, turning her face towards him, he kissed her, when they finished Grace said. No, no John, it's hopeless what chance have we, what future. No one is guaranteed a future Grace, all that matters right now is you and I, two people in love, blue skies, silvery sea, no matter what happens tomorrow or anytime in the future, we will remember this day forever, then a poem entered Johns mind.

Summer Love

1

Summer, Sunshine, the sea
Laughter, love, you and me
Walking along on the sand
Just you and I, hand in hand
Picnic at a quiet cove
Blue skies high above
Waves lapping on the beach
Heaven is within our reach
Summer, sunshine, the sea
Laughter, love, you and me

2

Summer, sunshine, the sea
Laughter, love, you and me
Drifting through a lovely summer's day
You and I in a carefree way
Swimming in the afternoon
Soft waves on the beach play a gentle tune
You say we'll always be as one
I kiss your face caressed by summer sun
Summer, sunshine, the sea
Laughter, love, you and me

3

The moon is shining high above
I am saying, it's you I love
The stars are shining so bright
I walk you home, we kiss goodnight
How happy we were on those summer days

But that was before you went away
Now there's nothing left for me to do
Just walk this beach and think of you
And summer, sunshine, the sea
Laughter, love you and me.

John Grace said that's beautiful, but the end is so sad. True Grace, but if he hadn't had those happy days of summer love, he wouldn't have had the sad ones, doe's one justify the other. What are you saying John that we should take all the love and happiness we can, when, we can.

That's right Grace we may never be given the opportunity again, they kissed again. Then grace said it's getting late we should be going. Grace and John drove up through the quiet village of Annestown, along the coast road to Boatstrand, they walked down to the dock wall to view the multi coloured boats mirrored in the water, then back up to the pony and trap and up the hill to Kilmurrin John stopped the pony at the top to view the scenery.

The Atlantic Ocean to their left, the Comeragh Mountains, a blue haze in the distance, the rugged wildness of kilmurrin cove below them, the scenic valley of Knockmurrin to their right, John said this is indeed a wondrous wild place. John that's what Bridget said you called it the day you were out the back strand. I did John said, and looking down on Kilmurrin Cove, from here, or out the back strand, they are the only words that describe this place.

They reached home at about five thirty, when Bridget heard them in the yard she came out to take Grace's bag and picnic basket. Did you enjoy your days work she asked John. I did indeed John answered, it was the most enjoyable days work I have ever experienced, John helped Grace down from the trap, held her close for a second Grace smiled and said thanks for a wonderful day. John said I'll untackle the pony, he's done a great days work, he has indeed Grace said and then went in to the house.

John made himself some tea, picked up the book that Grace had brought him and started to read for awhile, at about nine thirty he stretched himself, went over to the window and looked out, he saw Grace and Bridget sitting on the porch, he checked the water bucket it was half full, he picked it up anyway and walked out to the water trough. Bridget said it's a grand evening John, lovely John answered. Come and join us Grace said. John was about to go over when he heard a car coming in the boreen, it swung in the yard, Charles was driving and barely managed to stop the car about a foot from the water trough. As Charles got out of the car he staggered and then rested his hand on the bonnet, John saw Grace go inside.

Charles said well John how was your day. Grand, grand John answered. I forgot to tell you John, you and Patsy are going to the Quarry in the morning to help with the mobile stone breaker, take the Clydesdale and the large cart with you, and tell Michael Power I can only spare ye for one day. I'll tell him John answered. Charles staggered towards the door and went in.

Bridget came over to John at the water trough he's half drunk she said. It looks that way John answered. Did you see Patsy today. I didn't Bridget, I was supposed to meet him, but then I had to drive Grace in the pony and trap to Annestown. What a way to spend your Sunday off Bridget said with a grin.

The Quarry

John was awakened at about five by a cockerel crowing somewhere in the farm yard, he had set his alarm clock for about half five, now thanks to the cockerel, he didn't need it, he reached out to turn it off, and with his hands behind his head he lay there looking up at the ceiling thinking of the events of yesterday, he knew that since the first day he saw Grace that he had feelings for her, from the beginning they got on well together and enjoyed each other's company, but in his wildest dreams he didn't think that what happened yesterday would happen, he wanted to kiss Grace but didn't dare, and when they did kiss it was just wonderful, they say you will always remember your first kiss, he didn't know if yesterdays kiss was his first or not, but he did know that he would always remember it, she was a beautiful woman, but as she said she was married, but what happened on her wedding night ended her marriage even before it began, but she had to keep up the charade, but what future could he and Grace have, only stolen moments, he would settle for any moments with Grace, stolen or not.

John got out of bed, threw some water on his face, made some tea and had some brown bread that Bridget had made him, then walked out to the stable, took the winker's of the wall, went out to the field nearest to the yard, it was a beautiful summers morning, the field was covered in dew he could see the brown and white Clydesdale, she had been lying down but got up when John entered the field, John slipped on the winkers and led the horse to the water trough where she drank her fill, he then went back to the stable got the harness and the rest of the tackling and was soon backing the horse between the shafts of the cart, he went to the hayshed and filled a bag with hay and put it into the cart, the horse would need to eat something during the day, he was ready to go at twenty past seven.

Patsy arrived in the yard on his bicycle, and said to John I see you are ready to go. I'm waiting for you Patsy John answered. I'll be with you in a minute, I have to get a drink of water, there's a fierce thirst on me. Bridget was inquiring about you yesterday evening. I was suppose to meet her but I went to the village for a packet of fags, we started to play cards, one game led to another and before I knew it, it was closing time, I'm paying for it this morning, Patsy took a few slugs of water from the pump and then hopped on to the cart. John gave a flick to the reins and the horse moved out of the yard, John glanced towards the house he saw Grace standing at the window she waved her hand then she was gone from view.

They were making good time up the road towards the Quarry, around the crooked bridge and were soon approaching the blessed well. Patsy shouted at John to stop the horse, I must go in for a drink he said, he jumped from the cart, over the stile and into the well. John followed him, the well was large and circular with three steps leading down to it, beside the well was a whitethorn sceach with rags old and new hanging on it, what are those for Patsy John asked.

This is St Ita's well, although some call it St Bernard's, the history of this well is lost in the mists of time, for time immemorial people have been coming here for a cure, that's why it's called the blessed well, when Patsy was finished drinking, John knelt down on the step, cupped his hands dipped them in the water then raised them to his mouth and drank, he looked at his reflection in the water, now being distorted by the ripples made by his hands, who are you, he asked his reflection, where did you come from, what are you doing here, do you belong in this valley, have you been here before, where are you going, are these people your friends and neighbours or all strangers you got to know since April, the water was calm now, his reflection was clear, it looked up at him and started to recite a poem.

The Old Blessed Well

1

There's a cure in the old blessed well
That's what the old people tell
Between dusk and dawn is the time to go there
Kneel by the well and offer a prayer
To St Ita, St Bernard you take your choice
A prayer to both would be my advice

2

Out of the well flows a stream to the west
Dip in a cloth for the water is blest
Then with the cloth make the sign of the cross
Then hang it up on the whitethorn sceach
Visit twice more and you can rest assured
Any ailment you have will surely be cured.

Come on John Patsy called are you going to stay there all day, they got back in the cart and continued their journey past the blessed well cross, up the Manacaun hill and in the quarry gate. John brought the horse to a halt beside a man with an ass and cart he had a barrel of water in the cart. Patsy jumped out of the cart, saying I'll go and find Michael Power to see what work he has for me.

John spoke to the man with the ass and cart, who seemed to be about nineteen or twenty, the man said his name was Mick Duignan, that's a fine animal you have Mick said, not like my little fellow here. John said one of your little fellows ancestors did his bit for Christianity, what work is there here for an ass and cart.

Drawing this water Mick answered. What's the water for. The steam engine Mick said pointing across to where it was set up. John looked and saw the machine he had seen with Paddy and Patsy on Saturday evening, a belt was wrapped around the wheel on the side of the machine this belt was also attached to a wheel on the side of the stone breaker, smoke belched out of a funnel on top of the steam engine, a man with an oil can and cloth was standing at the machine.

John said I saw those two machines on Saturday evening and I'm sure that was the first time in my life I ever saw anything like them. Mick said when it's eight o' clock Bill Mullcahy, that's the man with the oil can will climb into that machine and pull a lever, that will set the wheel on the side in motion, and the belt on that wheel will turn the wheel on the breaker, but where in the world are you from that you have never seen a steam engine before.

A tall man wearing a hat and smoking a pipe approached John, are you the man Charles Arscott sent here. I am John answered, John Grey is my name. I'm Michael Power the foreman here, that's a fine horse and cart you have, you can draw the chips away from the breaker, draw them over to the far end of the quarry, did Arscott send someone up with you. He did John answered, Patsy Hayes, he went looking for you five minutes ago. If you see him before I do tell him to go up and feed the breaker. I will John answered. Where will I get these chips that, he's talking about.

I can see you never worked in a quarry before Mick Duignan said. Well the truth is John answered I don't know if I did or not. Come with me I'll show you. John walked over towards the breaker with Mick, he showed him a chute under the breaker, you back the horses cart under that, pull that lever there on the side and the chips will come down the chute, then close it off when the cart is full, I'll be over near the steam engine I'll keep an eye on you. Patsy came towards them three children walking beside him. John shouted at him I didn't know you had a family. I don't Patsy answered they are Michael Power's children. John said hello to the children, then he said to Patsy Michael Power said you must go feed the breaker. I know I met him. John heard a whistle blow, he saw Bill Mulcahy pull a lever, the large wheel on the side moved, slowly at first then picked up speed, the belt leading from the steam engine moved the wheel on the breaker and both machines worked as one.

The steam engine belched out smoke, John could smell burning coal in the air and heard the first stone being crushed and turned into dust and chips. He went and got his horse and cart, backed him under the breaker and watched until the holder was full, then pulled the lever and the chips rattled down the chute into the cart covering John with dust.

John was busy all morning over and back the quarry with his load of chips, he noticed Mick and his ass and cart come and go with water, and other horses and carts drawing the large stones up to where Patsy and another man fed them into the jaws of the breaker, he could see Michal Power walking around the quarry keeping an eye on everything.

At one o' clock he saw Michael put the whistle to his mouth and blow it but he couldn't hear it with the noise, he saw Bill pull the lever again, the engine and the breaker stopped, after the noise and din they had made, the silence seemed strange, but was soon broken by the voices of many men talking and taking their lunch bags from their bicycles.

Mick Duignan came over to John. You're doing alright he said, Patsy came over to join them and asked John had he brought anything with him to eat. I have nothing with me Patsy it never crossed my mind this morning to bring something with me. I have nothing either Patsy said I was late getting out of bed and didn't have time. Come on Mick said follow me, we won't let you starve. Wait till I feed the horse his hay, John got the bundle of hay he had left under a bush and gave it to the horse, he then got a bucket of water out of Mick's barrel, now he said he'll be alright for the rest of the day whatever about us.

John and Patsy followed Mick across the quarry to a large shed made from flattened tar barrels, a fire was lighting in front of the shed, several Billy cans were around the fire and the workers reached in and picked up their own, and found a place to sit then they took milk and sugar from their lunch bags, took the lid from their cans and put in the milk and sugar, John noticed that the lid was cup shaped into which they poured their tea. Have anyone of you got some bread and tea to spare for these two poor souls, who left home this morning without anything Mick asked. Several of the men offered John and Patsy some tea and bread, when they were all finished, fags and pipes were lit, some of the men started pitching coins into an empty Billy can, more sat around talking, John thanked Mick for getting them the food. Mick said they may not have much, but they won't let a fellow worker starve.

John noticed that Mick's hands were not like the hands of a labourer he asked, what do you do, when you're not drawing water to a steam engine. Oh anything I can get for the summer Mick answered. And in winter John said. I'll be back in college studying for the Priesthood. You are not a farmer's son then. No John, just trying to work my way through college. It's unusual for a vocation to knock on a cottage door I think it is Africa or South America for you Mick.

They were interrupted by loud voices coming from near the shed, two of the men were arguing, the argument turned to a scuffle, John and Patsy ran over and pulled them apart, just then Michael Power arrived. What's that all about he asked, someone answered they were arguing about Michael Collins and De Valera. Christ' Michael said I can't believe ye are still fighting the civil war, will it ever end, when your break is finished get two sledges from the shed there, they are some big rocks below in the quarry that need breaking, that should keep you quiet for the rest of the day, he then looked at John and said have I seen you before.

I was in Sullivan's Saturday night you might have seen me there. Yes Michael Power answered I saw you there, but apart from that I'm sure I saw you or someone very like you before. John said if you think of where you saw me or someone like me, let me know, it might help to solve the mystery of who I am.

If I remember I'll let you know Michael said and then he walked across the quarry towards the steam engine and breaker, as Patsy and John walked towards the breaker Patsy said would you think it strange if I said you look a lot like Michael Power, they heard the whistle blow again, they gathered up their bags and cans, placed them on their bicycles, the steam engine and breaker started up, the stones were again turned into chips, which John drew across the quarry all afternoon, he knew the chips would be used later to tar and chip the roads, some of the main roads had already been done, but the Co Council intended to do all the roads.

At a quarter to six John saw Michael Power blow his whistle, and everything stopped for the day, Patsy came over to John and they both went to say good bye to Mick Duignan. John said I suppose you will be here again tomorrow. I will he answered. Patsy said we are only here for one day. Glad to have met you John said, thanks for the help, and good luck with your chosen profession, most of the workmen were already leaving, bicycles strung along the three roads that led from the Quarry, John and Patsy got into the cart and were about to leave the Quarry when a lorry swung in the gate.

The lorry was carrying two strange looking machines, the driver backed the lorry up against a mound of chips, then climbed into the back of the lorry, turned something a couple of times at the back of one of the machines then a gust of smoke, and the sound of phut, phut, phut, phut, then the man sat up on the machine and reversed it on to a mound of chips and on to the ground. What in the name of God is that Patsy asked. It's called a dumper the driver answered, you are looking at the future here, the days of the horse and cart are numbered. John drove the horse out the gate and turned down the Manacaun hill. Patsy said I don't think the horse and cart need worry about those noisy auld things, they will never catch on, they turned right at the bottom of the Manacaun, as they approached the blessed well cross John noticed a makeshift tent erected in the wide margin at the cross roads, a donkey and a dog was tied to a sceach, a man was unloading dry straw out of the donkeys cart and putting it on the ground inside the tent.

Who's that John asked Patsy. That's rambling Pat, Patsy answered he travels all around the county he'll be here for a few days and then move on, if anyone want a chimney cleaned he'll do it, he makes grand tin gallons and mugs, people buy them for carrying the milk home from the farmers, he might cock a few fields of hay, or pull a few turnips, he comes around about twice a year surely John you have come across people like him before, they are part of the country side, sometimes one on their own, sometimes whole families, selling lino and rugs, little knick knacks for a halfpenny or penny. If I've seen the like of him Patsy I can't remember, as they continued their journey into Knockmurrin valley a poem came to John's mind.

Rambling Pat

1

He was sheltered from the North-east wind by high furze covered ditch
His donkey was tied to a blackthorn sceach, and also his mongrel bitch
The donkey's cart was painted green the wheels were black and red
Beside the cart a tattered tent, and inside a dry straw bed
An old black kettle was on the fire, the flames danced in the breeze
A blackbird sang in a nearby bush, the smoke curled through the trees
He sat upon a rotten log and asked me the time of day
He offered me his hand-made mug, said would you like some tay
I moved a stone close to the fire and sat down for a chat
He said his trade was travelling and to call him rambling Pat

2

The two of us sat round that fire in that grey frost covered vale
He lit his pipe, I sipped some tea he began his tale
I started life seventy years ago on sun-drenched summer morn'
To the sound of birds at the side of the road that's where I was born
I opened my mouth and breathed in God's fresh, free given air
My mother wrapped me in a coloured shawl, I travelled on from there
I've rambled around high mountains, and travelled valleys green
The beauty of this country, most all of it I've seen
I've knocked on doors, asked for food, offered to pay in kind
'Tis many a stone of spuds I've picked, and many a saddle shine

3

I've helped out at the threshing and cocked some fields of hay
I've danced till dawn, then pack my things, again be on my way
Down the road around the bend, some new place to view
An ass to buy, a pony sell, or clean a chimney flue
Sometimes I'd go from house to house mending pots and pans

And at the fairs I'd sell my mugs, and fine one gallon cans
I've slept outside on summer nights, the stars shining overhead
I've sheltered from the rain and snow, in some friendly farmers shed
I'd spin a tale to boys and girls as they sat on their mother's knee
The worker and his family, would always welcomed me

4

He poked the fire, threw in a stick, tapped his pipe on the log
And said soon I'll have to leave valley, mountain and bog
Failing health I'm getting old, they say I shouldn't be alone
But I'll do whatever I have to do to avoid an old people's home
I emptied my mug, said thanks for the tea, hope to see you again
I drove away, and waved my hand to one of the travelling men
A year has passed since I dined with him I wonder is he rambling still
And is his smoke curling up from the foot of an Irish hill
Or perhaps on some cold frosty morn' he failed to hear the fox's cry
And now his soul is rambling free through those heavenly roads in the sky

You might have thought you never saw, or heard of rambling Pat Patsy said, but that poem proves you either heard of him, or came across him somewhere. It was a quarter to seven when they entered Arscot's yard, Patsy picked up his bike and headed home, John untackled the horse, watered him and turned him into a field of good grass for the night, he went to the water trough, took off his shirt and washed the days dust off himself, Bridget came out.

Where's Patsy she asked. He's gone home John answered. Where was he last night. In the pub John answered. He wasn't the only one Bridget said. What do you mean. Charles was in a bad state last night he went out again after dinner and is not back yet. Where's Grace. She took the horse for a trot, about half an hour ago.

John put his shirt back on, I must go in and get something to eat I'm starved Patsy and I forgot to bring something to eat with us this morning. Ye're some egits, Bridget said, had ye anything to eat all day. Yes some of the workmen shared with us. I made some Shepherd's pie, Grace didn't want any, we'll never eat what's left, go in and get me a plate I'll put some on it for you. John got his plate and Bridget filled it up with a large portion, John took it inside sat at the table and cleared the plate, then made some tea, picked up a book, stretched on the bed and started to read.

Then he heard noise below in the yard, went to the window to see what was happening Arscott's car was stopped near the door, Arscott was standing in front of the car shouting at Bridget, where's Grace he asked, she's gone off on the horse Bridget answered.

Unexpected Guest

He turned around and staggered across the yard towards John, John could see him enter the workshop so he went out on to the landing, Arscott was struggling up the stairs holding a bottle of whiskey, John Grey he shouted, are you there.

I'm here John answered and went to help him up the stairs, Arscott but his hand around Johns shoulder and John guided him through the door and put him sitting on a chair. Have a drink Charles said pouring some whiskey into a mug, John took the mug and added some water to it, then sat across the table from Charles. Charles took a swig from the bottle do you like it here John he asked. It's alright John said. What do you think of the valley and the people here.

The valley's alright and so are the people, I suppose it's no different than hundreds of valley's like it in Ireland John answered, it has its sane and insane, its rich and poor, Catholic and Protestant, and not enough Christians, and most people struggling to put a crust on the table.

A crust on the table Arscott said, and work, that's all you ever hear the poor talk about do they ever think of anything else. It's a constant worry for them, trying to find work and to feed the family, and then after all their effort, they know their children will have to emigrate when they reached eighteen or nineteen, so you see Charles if they can't find work their children will starve that' why it's a priority with them. Things aren't that bad John. They are Charles, people are hungry here in Ireland, they have no work, and those who have work are on very small pay it's nothing short of slave labour. Nonsense said Charles. It's not nonsense John answered, I saw three children the other day in a turnip field, they were about ten or eleven years of age, bags tied around their knees, creeping over and back the field all day long, thinning turnips, pulling nettles and weeds for about three pence a drill, if that's not slave labour what is. That's the way it is here Charles answered, always has been and always will. No Charles John said you're wrong, up to now it's been that way, but better times are coming, plenty of work for everyone for good wages, the working class will be able to afford good houses and be able to educate their children, and walk tall among those who were once their oppressors. Oppressors, oppressors, Charles said we got rid of our oppressors when the English left.

Yes John said got rid of one form of oppression and replaced it with another, to the oppressed, it doesn't matter whether the oppressor is Irish or English they are still oppressed. Ah forget it Charles said here have another drink. What, are you celebrating, John asked. I'm not celebrating Charles answered, I'm drowning my sorrows.

What sorrows have you to drown you've got everything going for you, a fine farm, plenty of money. Money and land is not everything John. That's what the people who have plenty of it usually say, you have Grace I mean Mrs Arscott. Charles took another swig of whiskey and said, this farm and Mrs Arscott are the reason I'm drowning my sorrows, I never wanted this farm, never wanted Mrs Arscott, oh I wanted a Mrs Arscott all right, but not the one I have now, and the one I wanted, wanted me, I'm a city man, I love the city, I never wanted to leave it, one evening when I walked in at home my father, and Richard were waiting for me my father said come and join us, we are just discussing a new investment, a farm. I said we are going to buy a farm. We are not buying a farm we are acquiring one father said. I don't understand I said. A friend of mine, own a farm, he's in trouble in debt he's going loose the farm.

But I said, none of us know nothing about farming. We don't have to

Richard said, then my father said I think it's time you settled down, I have agreed a match for you, you and my friends daughter will be married, we will pay of the debt, and the farm is yours. I protested, who is this woman, has she any say in the matter. She will do what her father tells her Richard said, she loves the farm, it's all she's ever known, I'm sure you will get to like each other in time. I have a girlfriend I said, we've been together for a year now, we are planning to get married next year. Richard said you can never marry that woman she is below you, that woman is not for you, you can do better. John interrupted Charles and said, I thought all people were equal in the eyes of the Church.

Equal in the eyes of God yes, but not in the eyes of the Church, Charles answered, my father said if you don't marry Grace Mahony you will have no more to do with the business, you and this girl you've been seeing can shack up together see how you get on when you have to work for a living.

Wait a minute John said, you agreed to marry a woman you had never seen, why didn't you stand up to your father and Richard, why didn't you go with the woman you loved. I don't know Charles said I suppose I was too used to the soft life, too used to the money. John said so you left the girl. I never left her Charles answered, why do you think I go to town so often, but she left me last weekend, she said she had enough, she couldn't carry on, she said she had met someone else, they went to England last Saturday night.

You are selfish Charles, selfish, weak and pathetic, too weak to stand up to your family, you gave your marriage to Grace no chance, maybe you could have got to like each other, but you didn't even try, you sought solace in a whiskey bottle, and pleasure in another woman's bed, and now all you have is the whiskey and Christ, that is all you deserve.

Charles could no longer hear John, the empty whiskey bottle fell from his hand and rolled across the floor, Charles lay face down on the table, John picked him up and managed to get him down the stairs and across the yard, he shouted at Bridget, she came out to meet him, they helped Charles to his bedroom and laid him face down on the bed. Bridget walked back with John across the yard, he's in some state tonight she said he seems to be drinking more than ever, he was always fond of it, and abusive when he had too much in him.

Some people can take a drink Bridget and some people sure can't. I know John my mother use to say, what's in a man when he's sober, comes out when he's drunk. She could be right John answered.

John, remember the day we were in Kilmurrin. I do Bridget. I said I was going to England, and I wouldn't marry Patsy or anyone else, remember, do you think I was right. I don't know you could do worse than marry Patsy. I'll have to think about it Bridget said, as they stood there a full bright moon rose from behind the hill, John could see the shadows of the mountains and craters. Look Bridget said, you can see the man in the moon very clear tonight.

A small step for man, a giant leap for mankind John said. What did you say John. Something I heard or read somewhere, sometime. From your past Bridget asked. My past, my present, my future who knows, all I know is I heard it said, anyway it's a beautiful moon. Bridget said it is. John said, and someday man will go there. Go on Bridget said you're coddin me, how in the name of God could man go to the moon. John answered they will go there in a, in a. In a what, Bridget said. I don't know Bridget, it just won't come to me but I know for certain they will go there. Sure Bridget said and a woman will be Pope.

Turmoil

Grace had spent a couple of hours in Kilmacthomas shopping where she bought some new clothes for John. When she got home she said to Bridget I'm taking the horse to Kilmurrin for a trot. She had just passed Knockmurrin cross and took the west road out of the valley, and was out of sight when John and Patsy turned down by the forge on their way home from the quarry, her mind was in turmoil as she rode to Tankardstown cross, over to the coast road and down to Kilmurrin, she tied the horse near Murray's old thatch house, walked down across the stones and sat on a large rock.

Grace had a lot on her mind, a mind that had always been logical, anything she ever did was thought out and planned, her heart had never ruled her head, not until Sunday afternoon at Annestown bay when John Grey kissed her, and since that kiss her mind was in turmoil, she couldn't get John out of her mind, on the way to Annestown she had told John how she had met Charles and what had happened on her wedding night, but one thing she hadn't told John or anyone else, one night Charles had come home more drunk than usual, she was in the sitting room when he came in, he became abusive and demanded his rights as a husband, she fought him off, he hit her hard in the face she fell to the floor and remembered nothing else.

When she came around she was on her own, she knew that Charles had tried to have sex with her, whether he was too drunk to do it or not she was not sure, all she could remember was the punch in the face, she was glad she couldn't recall what happened because she would not have to live with the memory of him trying to molest her, she got off the floor and had a hot bath and put it out of her mind, never told anyone and never would.

The first day John came into the yard, she had been watching from the window, there and then she felt something she couldn't explain, the evening when Bridget came back from the cove, and she said she had been swimming and that John was there with her, she again felt something, Grace had never been jealous of anyone in her life, so she didn't know that her feelings that evening was jealousy, as she sat on the rock she thought of her home in the valley, she thought of how the farm was nearly lost, she thought of what she did to save it, she thought of her wedding night, if it hadn't been such a disaster would things have been different, she didn't think they would.

Grace got up of the rock and walked along the sand, she looked around the cove and up at the cliffs, out the entrance to the back strand, and thought John is right, this is a wondrous wild place, she asked herself what am I to do, I'm married to a man I don't love, and never will, I'm in love with a man I only met a few weeks ago. Before I met him, the farm, this valley meant everything to me. I married Charles so I could keep the farm and remain in the valley, and now all I want is Charles out of my life, I just have to get away from him if John Grey asked me to leave everything and go with him I would gladly do so.

Grace rode her horse up the valley road said hello to Paddy Casey as she passed the forge, went on up the hill and into the farmyard. Bridget came out when she heard her. Bridget Grace said you're in a bit of a fluster, what's the matter. It's Charles he came back very drunk, he went across to John. John carried him back I helped to get him up the stairs and on to the bed. Is he still there Grace asked. Yes he's asleep or unconscious. All right Bridget thanks now I must turn my horse out for the night, Grace took of the saddle, put it in the stable, walked the horse to the paddock, then back to the stable with the bridle, she closed the stable door and looked at her watch, quarter to ten she said out loud, she walked towards the house, half way across the yard she turned around and walked to the workshop, the door wasn't locked she entered and called John.

He answered and said come up. Grace went up, saw John at the table drinking tea. Will you have some he said. Yes please she answered. I hope you don't mind drinking out of a mug. Not at all, she answered. John said are you going to sit down or drink it standing up. Grace sat at the table, looked across at John and said I hear you had a visitor. A very drunken visitor John answered. What, did he want, Grace asked.

He wanted me to drown his sorrows with him. Sorrows what sorrows. It seems John said he has lost the love of his life. What, Grace said. Not you John said, some woman he knew in Waterford. Oh her, when he was in town he was supposed to be staying with Fr Richard. Supposed to John said but not, how long have you known. I've known for a long time. And you don't mind John said. Charles is a strong healthy man, he and I, we never, we never, you know. Never what John asked, never, are you teasing me, Grace said. John laughed you seem to find it hard to say you never made love to Charles. No I never made love to Charles.

John said yesterday in Annestown. Grace got up from the table and went around to John and said when we kissed yesterday, I've, I've thought of nothing else since, my mind, I'm all mixed up, I just don't know what to do, I need time to think, must go now it's getting late, Grace turned to go, John held her hand. Grace he said, yesterday happened because we both wanted it to happen, how can we walk away from it now. We can't Grace answered and we won't, now I've got to go, we'll talk tomorrow. John walked her down the stairs they kissed then John opened the door and watched Grace cross the yard.

The Creamery

John was in the workshop the following morning, when he saw Grace coming across the yard, as she came in the door she asked have you seen Billy. He's gone out with the cows John answered. Can you leave what you're doing for now John, I need you to take the milk to the creamery, I want Billy to take the mowing machine out of the shed and get it oiled up and ready, the weather looks settled, I think we will start cutting the hay tomorrow. John asked Grace, how is Charles this morning. Still asleep she answered, God John she said I don't know what I'm going to do, about what John asked. About Charles she answered, about you.

Grace John said I can't solve your problem with Charles, but if you have a problem with me I can solve that. How Grace said. If not being here would help, give you time to think, then maybe I should go. The last thing I want right now is for you to go. It seems to me Grace since I've been here thing have come to a head.

It may seem that way to you John, but it's not your fault that Charles's woman has left him, it's not your fault that the decision I made to save the farm was the wrong decision, it's not your fault that I have fallen in love with you, Charles is drinking more than ever and doing nothing, I nearly lost the farm before, now it is happening again, if what happened between you and I never happened, I would still need someone reliable around here to help run the farm, and I think you are as reliable as they come. Have you and Charles got joint accounts. We have John. Then what you need to do Grace is to open an account of your own, then Charles won't have control over all your money, would he notice. Charles has no interested in the farm or anything associated with it, no idea of the price of anything, he spends most of his time in town, except the odd day when he rides his horse around playing the part of a country gentleman, Charles won't know this place is in trouble until one of his cheques bounces, I think I'll do what you suggest.

John I, I want you to know I have always been in control of my emotions, always able to make what I thought was the sensible decision, but now when I see you, when I'm with you, nothing else matters, Charles, the farm, nothing I just can't think straight, if only I could go back to last Sunday morning when you were arguing with Fr Richard, I was in control, I was in charge, I should have never taken you to Annestown with me. Grace John said reaching out taking her hand, don't get upset, what happened, happened, we can end it now, walk away from it pretend it didn't happen. But it did happen I wanted it to happen, I want it to happen again and again, today, tomorrow, and forever.

John pulled Grace towards him, held her close, her head on his shoulder, they just stood there until they heard Billy close the yard gate. Grace took her head of John's shoulder and said John I don't know what to do, I need time to think, I know I want to be with you and when I'm with you I can put all thoughts of Charles from my Mind, but when I'm alone this voice says, you have a husband, stop this now, John Grey could be gone tomorrow, accept what you have and get on with it, put this love nonsense out of your mind. How can something that feels so good, be wrong.

Grace walked out to the yard, John followed her, Billy was walking towards the pump in the yard. Ah there you are Billy, Grace said, John is taking the milk to the creamery this morning, I want you to get the mowing machine ready for tomorrow, where's Patsy. John answered he went down the lane with some kind of yoke in the horses cart. Billy said that's a scuffler John he's taken it out to the turnip field. Grace laughed at John's description of the scuffler. Billy went over to the water pump for a drink. Grace said to John I must go in now, he'll be waking out of his slumber.

John went and got the horse and cart he had in the quarry, brought them over to the water trough, Billy had put the churns in the water to keep them cool, and now he helped John load them on to the cart. Do you think she's right to start cutting the hay tomorrow Billy asked. I think so Billy John answered, it's going to make a long hot summer. Then Billy said you and Mrs Arscott seem to be getting on well. We are Billy but she's an easy woman to get on with. She is that Billy said, she's some woman for wan woman.

John sat up on the side of the cart, Billy opened the gate, and John, horse and cart, went out the boreen, he decided to turn up the hill and take the high road to the creamery, John stood up in the cart going along the high road to get a better view of the scenery, to his left the Comeragh mountains looked clear and close, John's mind was dwelling on the mountain and stories that Paddy had told him about a highway man named Crotty, and how he would ride around the county raiding the rich to help the poor, after every raid he would return to his hideout on the Mountain, as John travelled along the high road he started to hum the words of a song, first the chorus, then the rest of the song.

The Legend of William Crotty

Chorus

Crotty the highway man though you are dead and gone
Your deeds they are a legend, your memory stills lives on
The sick, the poor, the needy you helped them on their way
You're a hero here in Waterford, still talked about today

1

There's a cave up in the Comeraghs near lake that's deep and cold
It was the home of William Crotty that highwayman so bold
From there he'd travel down to the Dungarvan / Carrick road
And he would wait for travellers, and relieve them of their load
Halt stand and deliver he would shout out loud and clear
As he robbed them of their riches they stood trembling with fear
Then he'd jump upon his horse and make his getaway with speed
And the money that was taken he would give to those in need
A gallant man on a horse of white, two pistols by his side
He robbed the rich to help the poor he was their hope and pride

2

He roamed around the county from Rathgormack to Tramore
And he was always welcomed at every poor man's door
The law tried hard to capture him they chased with gun and hound
But they couldn't get near him, his hideout couldn't be found
The bravest man, the fastest horse, the county ever knew
And to confuse those in pursuit, he'd turn the horse's shoe
They thought he was going to town when they found a fresh made track
But Crotty wasn't going to, but leaving old Kilmac
And high upon the Comeraghs, with a view down to the sea
Man and horse would rest awhile, away from company

3

To Kilmacthomas he would travel and mingle at the fair
He felt safe among them he had some good friends there
He'd have a drink with David Norris he was Crotty's trusted friend
But David Norris's wife would bring Crotty to his end.
At a place called Shanakill, there lived a man named Hearn
He spoke to Mrs Norris to see what he could learn
He bribed her into telling him the place of Crotty's cave,

And told her that in doing so, her husband she could save
She travelled up the mountain with Hearn by her side
Pointed to a cave and said there, that's Crotty's hide.
A week passed and she met Hearn, said the bird is in the nest
Hearn went and got his pistols and climbed up to make arrest.

4

He shouted out William a friend has come to call
Crotty then climbed out and was struck by a small lead ball
Though he was badly wounded, he was able to get away
He made his way to Norris's he was there the following day
Mrs Norris ran to Hearn, said Crotty's at our place
He is weak and wounded your shot hit him in the face
Hearn ran to Norris's sneaked up without a noise
Busted in the door, and took Crotty by surprise
Saying Crotty I arrest you in the name of the crown
And I am going to take you to jail in Waterford town.

5

They tried young William Crotty, you are guilty they said
The judge passed the sentence you will hang until you're dead
Crotty faced the hangman he stood tall and brave
And when they slipped the bolt, he went a hero to the grave
If you're ever on the Comeragh's, and the mist is coming down
And all is calm and silent, and you can't hear a sound
You gaze into the mist, at shadows big and small
And one of them reminds you of a horse and man so tall
Don't get too frightened if that shadow seems to sigh
It might be William Crotty as he goes riding by.

When John finished he stayed looking at the Mountain hoping that either the Mountain or the song might trigger something in his mind, but nothing came. When he reached the creamery there were a queue ahead of him, as he had never been at a creamery before and had no idea what to do, he decided to follow the man in front of him and go where he went.

The line of carts slowly moved forward, then John watched the man in front of him drive his horse and cart close to a high platform, a tall man with foxy hair was standing there, John heard the man in front of him say how ya Nicky. Nicky said a great day Jackie, then he took the churns and emptied them into a large tank, put the empties back in the cart the man drove the horse on, and Nicky waved John to the platform, saying I know the horse but I don't know you.

I'm John Grey. Nicky said I've heard of you, where's Billy today. Getting ready for hay John answered. Good weather for it Nicky said, I'm Nicky Casey. Glad to meet you John said.

When the churns were empty Nicky said are you going in for the butter. No one said anything to me about butter John answered. Billy always gets the butter once a week Nicky said, I'm sure today is the day he gets it, go around the corner there and in the door, Joe Kennedy will know if today is the day. Who's, Joe Kennedy John asked. Christ Nicky said, where, are you from, everyone know he is the manager.

John went around the corner and in the door, he saw a man sitting at a desk, I'm looking for Joe Kennedy John said. You have found him the man answered, who are you. I'm John Grey I'm working at Arscott's, could you tell me is today the day they get their butter, the manager looked in a ledger he had on his desk and said it is, he went and got the butter and gave it to John. John said thanks and went back to the cart turned right out of the creamery to go home by the blessed well cross. The horse plodded down Harney's hill, up by Kilbeg and soon John was turning left at the Blessed well cross, as he approached the blessed well he noticed a man unloading galvanised sheeting out of a horse's cart. John recognised him as Tommy O' Brien, one of the men who sang in the pub the night of the dance, Tommy also recognised John saluted and said. Anymore recitations. Now and then, John answered, another man came out from the well. Tommy said this is Jimmy Power. How ya he said. What, are you doing with the sheeting, John asked. Roofing the pump house, Jimmy answered. Pump house, John said, what, are you going to pump. A little petrol engine will be installed in this shed, it will pump the water from this well Jimmy said, up to the house in Kilbeg, the pipes have been laid it should be working in about two weeks.

A sign of the times Tommy said, running water and taps in all the rooms, indoor toilets, very handy. Very handy in winter Jimmy said, the east wind won't be able to take a bite out of your backside when you go to the toilet. I must be going John said. listen Tommy said a few of us are having a bit of a session in Cooney's pub on Saturday night, a few songs, a few tunes, will you come up and give a recitation or two. Get Paddy and Patsy to come with you. I'll say it to them to see if they are interested.

John was back in the farm yard around half ten took the churns from the cart and washed them, then backed the horse and cart close to the workshop door, loaded the gate he had mended on to the cart, as he was about to leave the yard Charles came out from the house and crossed the yard to John, saying I believe you carried me in last night. You had one too many John answered. What was I saying, Charles asked, I hope I wasn't, out of order. Some talk about the farm John answered nothing more. Charles looked relieved, anyway Charles said thank you for looking after me I'm off to town now I have some business to attend to.

Thinning Turnips

John took the gate out to the turnip field, they were three boys there thinning the turnips, the drills were soft Patsy had freshened them up with the scuffler, John watched the boys as they approached the headland, he thought to himself that's though work, pulling weeds, nettles, and thistles, when they came to the headland John spoke to them, that's hard work he said. The oldest looking boy said it was. Then John asked how much a drill, are you getting. Nine pence a drill the boy answered that's good, in other places we'd only get about sixpence for a drill this length, and they wouldn't be scuffled. Shouldn't you be in school, John said. We should, but the money is needed at home.

Did, you make that gate, the eldest boy asked. I repaired it John said. Could you make it the boy said. I could John answered. Are, you a carpenter. I am John said. I'm going to be a carpenter when I grow up the boy said. John admired the boy for his ambition, but knew it would never be fulfilled, education was only for the rich, these boys would be back here in the turnip field again next year, and the year after, and when they finished school, find a job on a local farm for a few years, then England or America.

John felt sorry for the boys, and thought it must be heart breaking for the all the parents in the country to see their sons and daughters take the boat, some of them never to return. John hung the gate, then took a tin of green paint from the cart and painted the gate at both sides, just as he finished painting he saw Billy coming out the lane with two horses pulling a strange looking machine.

What in heaven's name is that, John asked. It's a mowing machine

Billy said, and don't tell me you haven't seen one before. Well if I have I can't remember John answered walking around the machine, examining it and asking, how long will it take to cut the hay. I should be finished tomorrow evening Billy said, if the weather lasts we should be turning it on Saturday. John put the paint and brushes in to the cart, looked at the three boys, who were down on their knees again half ways across the field, and said to himself will things ever change for the poor of this Country.

Haymaking

About four o'clock on Saturday evening, John and Patsy were still turning the hay, Billy had left to bring in the cows for milking. Patsy saw the pony and trap coming across the field and said to John we have company, as the pony got nearer they could see it was Grace and Bridget, Grace was driving and stopped the pony beside John and Patsy. Grace said since ye agreed to work late Bridget and I thought the least we could do is bring you some tea and something to eat.

Bridget got out and Grace handed her a large teapot, Bridget took the food and two mugs from the basket, filled the mugs and gave them to John and Patsy. By God Patsy said to Bridget you'll make someone a grand wife. I will Bridget said if I can find someone who's interested all you're interested in is drinking stout and playing cards. Sit down here beside me Patsy said and who knows you might knock the bad habits out of me.

John walked over to Grace and said. Where's the wine. Grace said you know what happened the last time you drank wine. I do John answered and it was lovely, they were at the opposite side of the pony's trap to Bridget and Patsy. Is Charles back yet John asked. No Grace answered, he's been gone three days now, Father Richard is due out tomorrow he'll probably come with him. Grace John said the last time we spoke, you seemed uncertain about, well about us, are you having second thoughts, is there some doubt in your mind.

John one thing I have no doubt about is that I love you, that is one thing, I am certain of, but I must do what is right.

That's the question Grace what is right, or wrong, or who is to judge what is right or wrong, the establishment say you are a married woman and you must live with your husband for the rest of your life, and you can do that and swim with the flow, or you can swim against the current and say to hell with that, this is my life and I'm only going to get one shot at it, we all make mistakes Grace but should we have to pay for them for the rest of our life, if you end it with Charles, or if you don't, he's not going to give a dam one way or the other, he's going to carry on the same as ever, should you deprive yourself of a chance of happiness for someone like him.

John the way you spoke to Fr Richard on Sunday morning, no one from this valley would talk to a Priest that way, I don't know where you came from, but where ever it is they have more independence than we have and less fear, and are not dominated by the Church, if I swim with the flow, it will break my heart, if I swim against the current, they will do everything in their power to break my spirit.

Who are they John asked. The clergy Grace answered they run this country, oh we go through the farce of an election, but no law will be passed here unless the Catholic Church is in agreement with it, we have a Thaoisigh, and a President, but they are just figure heads, the Church is the boss, so for now John, it will have to be stolen moments for us. If it has to be stolen moments for now, so be it, but we will find away Grace if it's with the flow, or against the current, we will do it together. Will I see you later John. I promised Paddy and Patsy I'd go to the village with them tonight, but I'll see you before I go.

They were interrupted by a shout from the other side of the pony's trap Patsy and Bridget were rolling around in the hay. Ya big eiget Bridget said to Patsy, that's no way to look for a kiss grabbing a girl and rolling her around in the hay, if you want a kiss do it right and ask me out. All right Patsy said meet me at the Forge tomorrow evening and we'll go for a spin on our bikes. What about tonight,

Bridget asked. I can't tonight, I'm meeting Arthur Guinness. Bridget got up and brushed the hay from her hair and clothes. John said, if you want Bridget to take you seriously Patsy you will have to part company with Arthur Guinness. I would Patsy said if I thought she was serious about me. Grace said in a whisper to John, if it was only that simple for us.

Grace and Bridget gathered up the tea things and went back to the house, John and Patsy stayed turning the hay until seven o'clock. Patsy said I think we have enough done for today, John agreed with him, they both walked to the farmyard, hay pikes on their shoulders, Patsy got his bike and swinging his leg over the saddle said to John. I'll see you later. John said better enjoy your bottle tonight, if Bridget have her way you won't be getting many more of them. We'll see Patsy said.

John went in, washed and shaved, then fried himself some sausages and eggs that Bridget had bought for him from Jimmy Carey's mobile shop that came around twice a week, she also bought a pound of butter and a packet of Flahavan's porridge, John thought the mobile shop was a great idea, you didn't have to travel to the Village to get your groceries. John closed the workshop door walked across and knocked on Graces door.

Grace looked out the window and saw John, after a few minutes she joined John on the seat in the orchard. John said I didn't see Charles car in the yard so I guessed he wasn't back yet. No he's not Grace said. Maybe I shouldn't go to the village with the lads in case he comes home drunk. No John Grace said you go, he won't come back tonight, he'll come with Richard in the morning, anyway Bridget will be here with me, she has just gone down to Kathleen Casey's, she won't be long, you go John, Paddy and Patsy will be waiting for you, I'll walk with you to the road, the lane was peaceful, the sound of birds filled the evening air, rabbits ran for cover as Grace and John passed, as they left the yard Grace held John's hand, and said why didn't you come to the valley before I met Charles, I know together we could have saved this farm and be happy here.

Grace John said, I don't how or why I came to this valley when I did, but I know now I don't want to leave it, not unless you leave with me. Your memory John is there any improvement in it. No just the odd poem some I recite out loud and some I write in the note book you gave me. I don't want your memory to come back John I'm afraid if it does I'll lose you, if you remember who you are, where you came from, you won't be John Grey anymore and you would go back to where you came from, maybe to a girlfriend or a wife, God John, I couldn't imagine this valley without you, hold me John I'm afraid. John put his arms around Grace, she was trembling.

I 'm here with you now, we are together, none of us have a guarantee of tomorrow, let's take our moments of happiness when we can, God knows the world is full of so many sad moments, let's not spoil the happiness of the present by worrying about the future.

I'm sorry John I have never been in love before, and now I love you so much I want to tell the world, but I can tell only you, today I said it will have to be stolen moments for us but I want more than that, I want every moment with you, a day without you is just a morning drifting hopelessly into night with nothing in between. Grace john said a poem came to me the other night I wrote it down, it's called my Deise love, and as you are my Deise love, I want to read it to you, John took the poem from his pocket and started to read

My Deise Love

Chorus

My thoughts today wander over the foam
to you my love and my Deise home

I miss the Deise, my love I miss to
I must return to my Deise and you
I hope you are waiting I love you so
my love and my Deise to you I must go

1

Oh Deise my home the fairest of all
Though now far away I still hear you call
If I had the chance to go back through the years
I'd stay in the Deise with the one I love dear
She was everything to me and I loved her so
But from her and the Deise I had to go
Around this old world I destined to roam
Far away from my love and my own Deise home
My love in the Deise, is so dear to me
Her smile is as bright as the sun on the sea

2

Her eyes are as clear as a sparkling lake
Oh my sweet love many hearts you will break
My love and my Deise, my pride and delight
I'm so proud of you and the blue and the white
To you my own love none can compare
Just like the Deise, a jewel so rare
I've travelled the Deise from east to the west
Through lovely green valleys, to high mountain crest
From the wilds of the Comeragh, to the blue of the sea
Oh lovely Deise, you're heaven to me

3

My love's in the Deise, the place I call home
By the banks of your rivers I long to roam

The Suir and Backwater are so dear to me
Again watch the Mahon flow down to the sea
Your valleys and mountains to ramble once more
To walk once again along your seashore
The faces and places I saw as a boy
I think of them now with a tear in my eye
My love and my Deise, I'll praise you out loud
Because of you both I am ever so proud

4

There are many fair gems on this Island that's true
But none can compare to the Deise and you
As I sit here tonight I am thinking of home
And of you my own love far over the foam
My mind is made up I'm returning this year
To my home in the Deise and the one I love dear
When soft breezes blow in from the Ocean so wide
I'll stroll through green valley's with you by my side
When the birds in the summer sing their sweet song
With my love in the Deise that's where I belong

That's lovely John, but it's about going away, and I don't want you to go unless I going with you, Grace and John stood there in the lane clinging to each other, prolonging their moment together afraid the act of letting go would separate them forever, then they heard voices on the road and reluctantly let go, it was Bridget coming up from Kathleen Casey's, Grace and John walked to the road in silence, when they reached the road Bridget shouted Patsy's gone down ahead of you. John said to Grace, take this poem, for you truly are my Deise love, and I'll see you tomorrow.

A Session

John caught up with Patsy going down the hill, Paddy joined them at the Forge and the three of them cycled the sea road up to Kill village, there was a large gathering in Cooney's when they entered. The bar was about three feet below street level, small and pokey but cosy, a short counter to the left as you entered and an open fire on the right, John recognised some of the men from the quarry, and Nicky Casey the man he met at the creamery was sitting at a table with Andy Kirwan and two other men getting ready for a game of cards, they asked Paddy and Patsy to join them. Go ahead John said I'll get the drinks, John called for three large bottles of stout, took Paddy's and Patsy's over to the table and went back to the counter.

Taigh came in and took up a position near John at the counter. John said I thought we were coming for a sing song. It's early yet Taigh said give them a chance to wet their throat. John looked up to the end of the counter and saw Michael Power, the foreman at the quarry. Michael saluted and came down to them saying did you enjoy your day in the quarry. It was a change John answered and asked do they usually fight the civil war at dinner time.

Michael took a drink from his glass before he answered. Then he said the civil war left an regrettable stain on our tri colour, the best of men were lost on both sides, did you ever see a haggard after a threshing, all the chaff on the ground and the grain gone, men of vision gone, men who would not have caved in to the Church, men who would have caught this country by the scruff of the neck and hauled it up of its knees, if those men had lived to form a government this would be a great Country, not in the mess it is today.

Someone at the end of the counter said I think the Government are doing their best. Michael Power answered, tell that to the thousands of men and women that are emigrating, we have a strange way of getting our unemployment figures down, we export our youth. Did you fight in the civil war, John asked. No, Michael said, back then I was adjutant of the local brigade. Andy Kirwan was Captain and we gave six years fighting for our independence, I think that was enough it will take years to wash the stain of the civil war from the Tricolour.

They were interrupted by a shout from the card table, this bloody deck has five aces, how could anyone play cards with you lot, an argument ensued, some wanted to continue, some went to the counter to buy more drink, another man called on Martin O'Brien to sing a song, and that was the end of the card game. When Martin finished Nicky Casey sang, when the roses are in bloom down by the river, Patsy and a few more joined in the chorus, Tommy O'Brien called on John for a recitation. Come on John Taigh said, it will be interesting to see what you give us tonight.

I'm going to give a poem called strange country, it came to me last night I wrote it into the note book Grace, I mean Mrs Arscott gave me, I haven't it off by rote yet so I hope you won't mind if I consult my note book.

Strange Country

Sitting on a low wall that separated the pub car park from the beach, summer, somewhere in Ireland, children screamed and frolicked in the water, sand castles being built and knocked, Mother's rubbing on suntan oil looking for that elusive suntan, and hoping to avoid that not so elusive skin cancer, fishing boats out on the distant horizon, seagulls circling overhead, some people playing beach ball, others strolling hand in hand along the beach.

From the pub came the sound of singing and shouting, pints of beer,
whiskey, gin, and various other concoctions being consumed, all trying
to get high, all oblivious to the idyllic scene on the beach, I was feeling
good I rolled a joint, inhaled and exhaled, I was at peace with myself
and the world. I could see four men approach from the pub all of them
in a state of alcohol induced moranitis, they saw me and my joint one
shouted hey drug head, you shouldn't be smoking that, another said
shall we take it of him and stuff it down his throat.

Then a woman shouted from across the car park, leave him be and get
back here and buy some more drink, as they staggered back to the pub,
I thought to myself, they are full of alcohol, the most readily available
drug in Ireland, responsible for numerous road deaths, violence, broken
homes, and it's legal. And here am I sitting on a wall at a beach
smoking a joint, enjoying and admiring what the world has to offer,
and I'm breaking the law. Our Taoiseach opened a pub today our
minister for health closed a hospital ward, strange country.

There was silence for a few seconds when John finished, no cheer, no
clap. Then a man sitting at the fire said, Christ lad what kind of a
poem is that, that's not a poem at all, it doesn't even rhyme, and how
can you smoke a joint sitting on a wall, you might put a joint of
bacon up the chimney to smoke it, but it wouldn't do any good
sitting on a wall with it, and the minister for health is not closing any
hospital wards, with the scourge of TB he is trying to open as many
as he can, that's not a poem. It's a poem alright Taigh said, it's called
free verse. Free verse me arse the man said.

Well that rhymes Taidgh said, some of the men laughed, and Tommy
O Brien was asked to sing Bantry Bay.

Thanks Taigh John said you came to my rescue there. Where in the
name of God did you get that poem Taigh asked. From where ever I

got the rest of them. No Taigh said that poem is completely different from the rest, it mentions Ireland, it mentions the Taoiseach, only for that you would never think it was about Ireland, where would you see anyone smoking a joint in Ireland, in Jamaica maybe, in the jazz clubs of New Orleans or maybe in the Orient, but not in Ireland. And mothers on the beach with suntan lotion, maybe in the south of France, sure they can't afford a pint of milk here, not to mind suntan lotion, and people being killed on the roads, I have never heard of anyone being run over by a Horse and cart, a few bottles of stout on Saturday night, that's not going to kill anyone, as for the Taoiseach opening a pub, if he even thought about it Arch bishop Mc Quaid would belt him over the head with his Crozier.

All right John said I still believe it came from the same place as the rest of my poems. I've been enquiring about your poems John, I'm a teacher and I've never heard of your poems, I've asked some of my colleagues and they never heard of them, the last night we met over in Sullivan's you spoke about time travel.

I have no doubt John all the poems I've heard you recite are about our present time, apart from the one you gave tonight, do you know what I think John, and call me crazy if you like, I think they were written by someone in the future, someone looking back at the past.

That's impossible Taigh, and what about tonight's poem. That was written by the same person Taigh said, but when he wrote that he wasn't looking back, he was writing about his own time in the future. God if that is true, and if that is the future I'd rather not go there.

You can't be serious Taigh John said. I'm very serious John, let's look at the facts, you come into the valley no memory, no idea who you are, no one here knows you, it seems you are a qualified carpenter, you can read and write, and recite poetry.

Some of the young men here of your age can barely read, some of them can't read at all, and they certainly can't recite poetry, you are not of our time John, or else you are not of our country, and yet your accent say you are one of us, I'm baffled John.

John took a piece of paper from his pocked and put it in the top pocket of Taigh's jacket, have a look at that sometime and tell me what you think of it, it came to my mind the other night I wrote it down and another one about the council men. There's a good few council men here Taigh said, maybe they might like that one to make amends for the last one, all right lads Taigh said John was in the quarry the other day and now he's going to recite a poem about the council men and this one rhymes.

A Council Man Remembers

1

Today is my last day working I've been pensioned of at last
But I'd like to tell you all the way it was back there in the past
You know I've been a council man for forty years or more
Every day at seven I would be heading out the door
Up at six each morning, the fire was burning bright
Sure you know we had no gas then, or know electric light
The flickering light of a candle through shadows around the room
I'd sit and eat my breakfast in the early morning gloom
I'd have an egg if I was lucky, and some homemade bread
Made in the auld oven pot, 'twas the best I've always said

2

Then I'd get my Billy can, and hang it on the bike
The shovel on the crossbar, I had it bound up tight
I'd swing upon the saddle and head off with my load
The tyres would leave their mark in the grey frost on the road

Ten miles or more to travel before my work would start
In the early morning silence now and then a dog would bark
Then I'd meet up with other lads, John, Pat, and Mike
All day long we'd cut and clean along those dreary dykes
On the quite country roads, clearing blocked up drains
You knew the friendly houses, where to shelter from the rain

3

Then sometimes to the quarry, to break and shovel stone
The east wind blowing around you would chill you to the bone
Then would come the summer, the days were fine and long
The birds were whistling loudly, the Cuckoo sing his song
Spreading dust along the road out of a Horses car
And wondering come the weekend, could you afford a jar
The children coming home from school, would stop and have a chat
They would gather around the Horse, and give his head a pat
You would travel around the county, when you were a council man
And at times you had to sleep in a cold and draughty van

4

The Billy cans were boiled up, time for a rest and joke
Sit on the ground and drink your tea, strong with the taste of smoke
Have a game of pitching, throwing pennies in the can
And arguing about politics, and who's the better man
All day long you worked, from early morn to night
Your friends would share a fag, or maybe fill you pipe
The council men are scarce now, machines are in their place
But the roads around the county are all in some disgrace
I never saw such potholes, and the fences are all wild
Ah God be with the old ways, the auld shovel, hook, and scythe

There was no silence this time when John finished the poem a loud cheer went around the pub. Michael Power said I see you are no stranger to the ways of the council man. I don't know about me John answered, but whoever wrote the poem seem to know. Taigh said to John that poem proves my point. How John asked. A line in the poem says, you know we had no gas then or no electric light.

So John said. Taigh answered, the poem doesn't say we have no gas now, it says we had no gas then, past tense, someone looking back, and at the end of the poem it says council men are scarce now, they are not scarce. Taigh turned to Michael Power and asked how many men have you working Michael. Michael answered, twenty.

And every other overseer have about the same Taigh said, and machines are in their place, that line makes no sense, how can machines take the place of council men. Johns said when we were in the Quarry the other day two machines called dumpers came in, the driver said they would replace the horse and cart, if machines can replace the horse maybe they can replace men as well. Taigh said I doubt it John, I'm convinced your poems are written by someone in the future, looking back at the past.

But that is impossible John said, if my poems are from the future, I must be from the future, if I am how did I get here, where is my time machine, how do I get back to the future, had no gas, have no gas, that could be a printers error. The sing song that was going on came to a sudden stop, and everyone was looking towards the door, someone said it's Guard Donlon. John turned and saw a heavy man with a moustache standing in the doorway. Everyone out he said, it's gone the time, ye are breaking the law. The proprietor started shouting time please, time please, some of the customers headed for the door, others took a last quick slug from their glass before they left.

John, Paddy and Patsy went towards the back door. Where are ye going the guard asked. Out the back for our bikes Paddy answered. I hope ye all have lights on them. We have guard, they all answered together, when they got outside John said. But we haven't any lights. Never mind Patsy answered, go fast while he's still in the pub. The three of them turned over towards the Chapel just as the Guard came out the door of the pub. Halt he shouted, but it was too late, they peddled over the street, down the Manacaun hill, past the blessed well, and were soon at Knockmurrin cross. John put the bike inside the gate, Kathleen would want it in the morning for mass, John and Patsy walked up the hill together, and at the entrance to Arscotts he said goodnight to Patsy and went in the boreen.

Mass

John was up at nine o'clock Sunday morning, lit the stove and put the kettle on, then washed and shaved he cut a slice from a large pan loaf, stuck a fork in the slice, opened the door of the stove bent down to make toast, he was in that position when Grace walked in. John she said Charles is not home yet, Father Richard will be saying eleven o'clock mass in town they'll probably come after that, would you mind if I asked you to get the pony and trap ready to drive me to mass. Grace John answered ask me to drive you to the moon and I'll do it, you and I travelling the Milky Way together, we'll stop for a drink on Venus, and stay overnight on Jupiter. John be serious Grace said. John asked what's wrong, Grace. Mass she answered. What's, wrong with going to mass. Nothing she said, it's, it's, what happened between you and I. I wonder should I go to mass.

Why ever not Grace you have every right to go to mass, God never said the road to heaven would be deprived of happiness, by all means go, and when you go into the chapel and kneel down, remember you are not kneeling among saints, every one there will have something on their mind, whether it's something they should have done, and didn't, or something they did do, and shouldn't, we all have to go through this world the best way we can, none of us have the right to judge others, only God can judge us and I have no doubt he will when the time comes.

John Grace said you say strange things at times, sometimes I wonder if you believe in God at all, and then you say something like you just said.

Oh I believe in God alright, but the God I believe in is a Christian

God and he wants to save all mankind, not just the chosen few, now Grace John said you go across and get yourself ready, and when I finish my breakfast I'll get the pony and trap ready, and we'll drive stately to the chapel together, and when we get near the village you can link your arm around mine lay your head on my shoulder, and before you alight from the trap give me a kiss on the cheek and in doing so you can inspire the Priest to give a hell and damnation sermon.

Grace laughed at the thought of it and said wouldn't it be grand if we could. John knelt down to the stove again saying I better toast this piece of bread or we'll never get to mass, John said come down here for a minute I want to tell you something. Grace pulled her dress above her knees and knelt down beside John. What, do you want to tell me, she asked. Oh nothing earth shattering he answered just something truthful and natural, I love you they kissed there on the floor. When they finished John said your lips are a lot warmer than this stove, can you kiss this piece of bread and turn it to toast. Grace got up tossed John's hair playfully and went across to get ready for mass.

The pony trotted willingly towards the chapel, as they got nearer they met some more ponies and traps and a few motor cars. Grace said to John the motor cars are more plentiful now, soon the pony and trap will be obsolete. John answered there are big changes coming Grace, but for the better. When they reached the chapel John got out and tied the pony to an ash sapling on the ditch, then caught Grace by the hand helped her down and did an exaggerated curtsy. A young man passing said, why not go down on your knees in front of her. John answered. I did that earlier this morning. John saw Paddy and Patsy at the chapel gate. He said to Grace I'll go in with Paddy and Patsy, he whispered remember you are not among saints.

Paddy was having a last pull on his pipe before he ventured in. Patsy asked John are you coming hunting with us after dinner. I don't know John answered I'll see, John didn't want to commit himself he was hoping that Grace and himself might be able to spend some time together in the afternoon. John, Paddy, and Patsy went into to mass several men were standing at the door. John looked up the chapel and noticed that the men were at one side of the chapel and the women at the other, for some reason this didn't seem right to him, he asked Paddy, why are the men and women sitting separately.

Paddy gave him a strange look and said are you feeling all right, that's the women's aisle to the left, and the men's to the right, and that's where they always sit, how can you have men and women sitting together at mass. John was also surprised that all the women were wearing either a head scarf or hat. The Priest went to the pulpit to give his sermon. John asked Paddy his name. I don't know Paddy said he must be a missionary I haven't seen him before. John listened to the sermon it was all about sins of the flesh, and that people who committed such sins would burn in hell, that dance halls were a place of temptation, and that the local Priest should patrol the halls to make sure that the devils work was not happening there, and that parishioners should only attend card drives that were organised by the Priest. It is well known that the devil is an ardent gambler and has sat down at many a card table.

John dipped his finger in the holy water font blessed himself and walked out. Paddy and Patsy soon followed. God Paddy said did you hear what he is on about, it's a good job he wasn't at the last dance if he saw Patsy doing that waltz he'd have him doing penance for six months. Why is it Patsy asked that the only bit of enjoyment the working man have, a game of cards, a few bottles of stout on a Saturday night, the odd dance, why are we condemned from the pulpit every Sunday morning, sins of the flesh the Priests are always on about sins of the flesh, do they think that is all we think about in our daily struggle to exist, an auld dance and a laugh with a girl, it's about the only bit of enjoyment we get, and the Priest telling us it's sinful, and we'll burn in hell, debauchery, that's another favourite of theirs, and most people don't even know what it means, I wonder where in this parish would I find someone to debauch me, sins of the flesh, do they ever think of anything else, it can't be healthy for them.

Patsy took a packet of gold flake from his pocket. Paddy said that's right Patsy light a cigarette and cool off, John said the day will come when the Priests themselves will almost ruin the Catholic Church. How will they do that Paddy asked, I suppose you could call it sins of the flesh John answered. What Patsy said Priests commit sins of the flesh, never, they might give us a roasting about it on Sunday, but they are holy men John they would never do anything like that.

John said remember when we were talking about the all Ireland in the pub and I said I had a vision that Waterford would win it in fifty nine, well sometimes late at night when I'm asleep, or maybe I'm awake, is it possible to dream when you're awake, anyway I hear these voices at the side of my bed. What kind of voices Paddy asked. Men, sometimes women talking John answered, they are talking between themselves and l think to me, last night they were talking about the Bishops covering up sexual abuse on children by some of the Priests, and at the other end of my room I could see a headline on some ones paper and it read, Cardinal deny child sexual abuse by Priests, and then someone came into the room and said visiting hours are over and the voices and vision ended.

God John Paddy said that's wicked talk all together don't repeat that to anyone, if the Priest hear you talking like that he'll but a curse on you. I can't understand it Paddy, where are these visions coming from, awhile back I had a vision of two huge towers being hit by an aeroplane and they collapsed killing thousands of people, the sea rising up somewhere in Asia and doing untold damage, their conversation was ended by the people coming out of mass. John said to Paddy and Patsy I might see you later. John was waiting at the pony and trap for Grace she had two elderly women with her. She said to John this is Mrs Walsh and Mrs Power, they are coming down the road a bit with us. John said hello to the women and helped them into the trap.

John turned the pony and trap and they trotted away from the chapel, the two women were talking about the Priest, they wondered what he would be like to go to confession to, and what kind of penance he would give. John thought to himself, what in the name of God would these two innocent women have to confess, and wasn't their every day existence penance enough without getting more from a Priest, half way down the Manacaun hill Grace asked John to stop the pony. The women thanked Grace for the lift then got out, John flicked the rains and the pony moved on.

Well Grace John said you survived. I did Grace said but it wasn't easy listening to his sermon, the devil at card games, Priest's patrolling dance halls, sins of the flesh, we have no hope. Don't mind him Grace, he's just trying to get people to believe, if he preached about love and peace, instead of hellfire and damnation his message might be accepted easier.

A New beginning

1

Daffodils and primrose, heath in the sun
The world is awaking, springtime has come
The winter is behind us, summer to the fore
Birds all are singing and nesting once more
Buds on the trees, the fields fresh and green
Darkness defeated, light rules supreme

Everywhere you look, life pours from the ground
The laughter of spring can be heard all around.

2

New hope comes to us all this time of year
And belief in the future now that Easter is here
Spring and Easter, Easter and spring
To a stagnant world, a new life they bring
A new beginning, an exit from despair
God has save us let us give thanks in prayer
We are born, we live and die but we are not lost
Because God sent his son to die on the cross

3

Good Friday he died on Mount Calvary
He gave up his life so we could be free
They went to the tomb on the first Easter morn
To find Christ had overcome the cross and the thorn
Easter has come and mankind is saved
Jesus the saviour has risen from the grave
The tomb it is empty, he walks with the living
To all of mankind a new life he has given.

Sorry grace John said when it came to my mind, I had to say it I still have hope, that one of my poems will connect me with my past. Grace said I was wondering about your poems, do you think it's unusual for a, well a working man to be quoting poetry. Maybe it is now Grace but back in the mystic mists of time everyone listened to the poets and bards, that's how our history and heritage was passed down to us, the poets wrote about great events and great heroes, and travelled Ireland reciting their poems, and the ancient Irish listened.

But why have people abandoned poetry, why so few reading it now Grace asked. I'm not sure John answered, I think it became elitist and got confined within the walls of academia, where a few within an inner circle write so called poetry which no one can understand only themselves, it reminds me of the King's new suit of clothes, everyone went along with the farce afraid to look stupid, but the innocence eyes of a child saw it for what it was, a con job, maybe we should get the opinion of the children on some of this modern poetry, no Grace the ordinary people of Ireland never abandoned their poets, it was the poets abandoned them.

John stopped the pony at the stable door and Grace got out, Bridget was at the pump washing spuds for the dinner, Charles and Richard hadn't arrived yet, he led the pony out to the paddock and went upstairs, he put some fire wood in the stove went down stairs again to the spud house and choose a few nice size spuds for his dinner went up and put them in a saucepan on the stove.

He heard a car drive in the yard, he went to the window and saw Charles car, Richard was driving, he saw Richard get out and go around to the passenger side, open the door and help Charles out, Grace came out to meet them and she and Richard helped Charles indoors, Bridget met them in the hall and helped Grace get Charles upstairs.

Fr Richard went into the sitting room and helped himself to a whiskey. Grace joined Richard we managed to get him to bed she said, will you stay for dinner. If you don't mind Grace I will. Fr Richard Grace said what's come over Charles, he hasn't been home now for days, he's drinking more than ever, and when he is here he's no help around the farm. Oh don't worry Grace, it's just a phase he's going through, he'll pull out of it one of these days give him a chance, his life has changed completely since he married, he was always a City man, now he must get used to country life, he'll come around wait and see. Where was he the last five days.

Fr Richard took a sip of his whiskey, before he answered. Sometimes he stayed with me and sometimes with friends. I'm worried Grace said. Oh you have nothing to worry about you have a fine place here it's going well. It was going well before until my father lost his way and you know what happened then, I'm afraid the same thing might happen again.

Nonsense Fr Richard said, but he could see Grace was worried, Grace he said I'll talk to Charles, I'll come out when he's sober, he's just finding it hard to adapt to country life he misses the town and his friends. I think he's missing one friend more than the rest Grace said, maybe we should have never married I think it was a mistake. No not a mistake Fr Richard said it's, well it takes time for two people to adjust to each other, anyway you are married now you will just have to make the best of it, there's no going back, give it time and I'm sure everything will work out all right, now Fr Richard said let's have dinner and then you can drive me back to town. I can't Grace said I'm only driving a few weeks and I've never drove in town. But I have to get back I have some friends calling at four.

Can't you drive Charles car back in. No, no Richard said I'm sure Charles will need his car, how could I get it back to him, Bridget had entered the sitting room to call them to dinner and heard the conversation. She said I couldn't help but hear John can drive. John Richard said, you mean the carpenter, but where on earth did he learn to drive, where, would he have had access to a car. I don't know Bridget said, he was looking at Charles car one day and I asked him could he drive, he said he had drove bigger and faster cars than that. I can't have him drive, the way he spoke to me the other Sunday, him and his one God for everyone, did you ever hear such nonsense, we'll end up at each other's throats before we reach town.

Grace said would it help if I came with you, I could sit in the back and keep the peace. Oh all right Richard said if that is the only way I can get to town I guess I have no choice. I'll go and tell him Bridget said. No, no Grace said you prepare the dinner. I'll go across and ask him. Ask him Fr Richard said don't do any such thing, go across and tell him, he is your employee. Well Fr Richard Grace said, it is his Sunday off, and he's already drove me to mass this morning. Fr Richard said he should be thankful he has a job, if he wasn't working for you he would probably have to emigrate, but do what you have to do.

Grace crossed the yard and went up the stairs John was sitting at the table eating his dinner. How are things on the domestic front, he asked. Charles has gone to bed, Richard and I are about to have dinner, John will you drive Richard to town later. I'm not driving him John answered. John Grace said this is a chance for us to be together this afternoon, he asked me to drive, but I have no experience driving in town, Bridget said you could drive, he wasn't happy with that, I said I'd go with you to keep the peace, he must be in town before four o'clock, if we leave at three we will have the rest of the afternoon together. All right John said, but will you ask Bridget can I borrow her bike I want to go for a swim, I'll make sure I'm back at three.

Suspicion

John arrived at the cove at about one thirty, put on his togs and sat on the beach for awhile, he didn't want to swim too soon after his dinner, there were a few people scattered along the beach, mostly mothers and children, not too many men, two boys came over to John and said hello. John recognised them as the boys he met in the turnip field, this is better than thinning turnips he said to them, they laughed and said it was, can you swim he asked them. We can they answered. And why aren't you

We're waiting for Sean to come back. Who's, Sean John asked. You met him the other day, they said, he was thinning the turnips with us. John remembered the third child and asked, where, is he now. He went out the back strand with one of the Priests from the mission to pick Dilisk. John sat up straight, he was worried, but he didn't know why, he got up, and looked towards the back strand, something's wrong he said what is it, why can't I remember, then he thought of his conversation with Paddy and Patsy after mass. Again he could see the headline on the paper, Bishop denies child sexual abuse by clergy, he ran towards the water dived in and swam towards the back strand, climbed up to the entrance and out through it, he stood there and looked around, he couldn't see the Priest or the boy, he ran down to where the caves were he saw the Priest and the boy near the entrance.

The boy had his swimming togs on the Priest had his shoes and socks off, the legs of his trousers rolled up around his knees they were standing in about a foot of water picking Dilisk. John felt a great relief come over him, he shouted are you alright Sean. The boy turned around and said we're picking Dilisk. The Priest said to John he's a great lad to help me. Sean John said your friends are waiting for you. I must go now Father, Sean said and ran up the beach. John said do you think Father it's wise for you to be out here alone with a young boy. The Priest answered why not, I don't see any harm in it. Maybe not John said but I think you should be more careful in future. Why the Priest asked, then his expression changed, you don't think, good God man I'm a Priest, how could you think I would do anything to a child. I don't think you would Father, but you could be leaving yourself open to accusations in the future.

My God he answered, what kind of mind have you. I was just thinking of the welfare of the child Father, I'm sorry if I misread the situation. I don't know who you are the Priest said, or how you know about such things, or who's putting these thought's in your head, what filthy books have you been reading, the censorship laws in this country are not strong enough, maybe someone is sending you these books from England, all such books should be burned. I haven't any such books Father, and if I had, you would have no authority to burn what's mine, I must be going now I'm sorry if I misjudged you, it's better to be safe than sorry, there are a lot of predators around Father. Are you saying we have such people in our Church, how dare you, how dare you make such an accusation. I am not accusing anyone Father, but when I heard that you were out here alone with a child I had to make sure the child was safe. Of course he was safe, what kind of person do you think I am, good God man what you're saying is scandalous I'm going to report you to the parish Priest. John said do what you have to do then swam back to the beach, he saw the three children playing and enjoying themselves, with other children. He dried and dressed himself, cycled back to drive Richard to town. Grace and Father Richard were ready to go when John arrived, Grace handed John the keys of the car and she then sat in the back seat. Father Richard came out closed the hall door behind him and sat in the passenger seat.

Seaside Visit

They drove in silence for awhile, then Grace asked John if he enjoyed his swim, John answered that he did. Fr Richard asked him if they were many there. John said not too many and added I met one of the Priests from the mission. Was he swimming, Fr Richard asked. No John said he was out the back strand with a young boy. What Fr Richard said. Oh don't worry, it was all quite innocent this time, they were picking Dilisk. Nothing unusual about that what else, would they be doing Fr Richard said.

What else indeed John said, I believe you have a problem with some Priests and young boys. How would you know of such things. I'm not sure Father I must have heard it, or read it somewhere. You could not have read about it. John asked is that because it's not happening, or because it's been covered up. I have no idea of what you're talking about, or where you are hearing these things, we in the Church have our own way of looking after our own. I have no doubt you have but it is the wrong way, it will do the Church enormous damage, you know what a bad apple can do to the barrel. We, have no bad apples Fr Richard said. John said what was it that Jesus said, something like, he that harms the little ones, it would be as well for him to have a millstone tied around his neck and cast into the depths of the sea, well if he was here today someone could make a good living supplying him with millstones.

What are you two talking about Grace asked I can't hear with the noise of the car. Fr Richard answered, John thinks the Church is involved in some conspiracy that will damage it in the future, the Church was never as strong in Ireland as it is now, we have hundreds of vocations every year, we are sending Priests to South America,

Asia, to South Africa, they are spreading the word of God all around the world. The majority of them are, John said but some are damaging the Church, some of those countries ye are sending Priests to now, will in the future have to send Priests here. That's ridiculous, no Priests here in Catholic Ireland, what foolish talk is that, don't make me laugh. Fr Richard, said I don't know where you get your strange ideas from but I think you better leave the running of the church to us, and you look after your carpentry, Fr Richard turned to Grace and said where on earth did you find this man, did you hear the strange notions he have in his head, Priests damaging the church, no vocations in Ireland, utter nonsense, whatever will he say next.

Fr Richard directed John to his house, when John stopped the car, as he got out he said to Grace I'll drive out tomorrow and talk to Charles don't worry, I'm sure everything will be alright, now you sit in here and try and talk some sense into this man, then he walked towards the house and waved to Grace and John as they drove off.

John Grace said, what do you mean, Priests damaging the church. It's some kind of vision I had Grace, I was telling Paddy and Patsy about it, voices in my head headlines on a paper about the Church covering up sexual abuse by Priest's on children. God John I can't believe that could happen, not here in Ireland, the Priest's are always condemning sins of the flesh, they would never interfere with a child. Maybe that's the problem Grace, it sounds so outrageous that no one will believe it, ah let's forget it and not spoil the rest of the day. Grace moved closer to John and said let's drive out to Tramore.

As they approached Tramore Grace said, we'll drive to the far end of the prom and go for a walk on the beach, it should be quiet there. I'll show you the way. I know the way John said. Have, you been here before. I don't know John answered but I definitely know the way. John parked the car at the far end of the prom, the tide was out, a large crowd was on the beach in front of the prom, some swimming, some relaxing in the sunshine, Children screamed and ran here and there, as they walked along the quiet end of the beach Grace held John's hand. Charles, haymaking, the farm, tomorrow, nothing else in the world mattered, just the fact that she and John were walking the beach together hand in hand. The farther along the beach they went the quieter it got. John picked up some flat stones and skipped them along the water Grace took of her shoes and walked bare foot on the sand. I love the summer grace said it's my favourite season. Summer John said the teenage season, did you know the seasons of the year can be compared to the seasons of our life.

Life and Seasons

1

Spring when sap stirs in the trees, and all things begin to grow
Warm sun creep into corners to melt the last of winter snow
Now the ever increasing chatter of birds, tell us once more its springtime
Hibernating animals awake from sleep, and emerge into warm sunshine
They gaze in wonder upon the world, like a baby's first view of life
A life that lies tantalising ahead, with all things good, no thoughts of strife
Spring, the baby of the season, when everyday bring something new
Blossoms bloom, trees grow green, and baby's growing too

2

Summer, and all its energetic activities, so many happy hours
First love and kiss, and the world sparkles like sunshine after showers
Long summer days drift into short summer nights, two hearts beat as one
Birds in an all day search for food, to feed their ever hungry young
Season of colourful flowers and happy hearts, dancing, singing, seaside play
Birds, bees and other summer sounds form a choir to us sing through the day,
Summer the teenage season, when the world is perfect, and so many things to do
The Cuckoo is going, the cornfields turn to gold, and summer is going too

3

Autumn coloured golden brown, ripened fruit is picked for store
Swallows in line along the wires are preparing to fly away once more
Autumn evenings, the scent of bonfire smoke, we go walking kicking leaves
The squirrels are busy gathering nuts, as they run from tree to tree
The corn is cut and saved, days grow short and nights grow longer
Our summer love has born its fruit, and everyday grow big and stronger
Autumn, season of middle age when hair turns grey and life slow down
Then a cold gust of wind and the last clinging leaves fall to ground

4

Winter comes, the world takes on an empty look, fields are bare and still
We sit by the fire our world now consists of a window view of a nearby hill
The first frost and snow, days of pension books and pills, all is damp and cold
Days now spent from bed to fire, limbs now aching, tired and old
Dark winter days spent in loneliness, with just memories of the past
Now the final realisation, life is just a passing phase, nothing is made to last
Winter, season of old age, waiting for the day when this world and I will part
And when God calls, hopefully in heaven another spring will start.

Summer John, I love it, what did you call it, the teenage season, season of colourful flowers and happy hearts, dancing, singing and seaside play, that's what I want to do John, dance, sing and frolic on this beach and be happy with the man I love, but I can't I'm a married woman, and if I start dancing and singing and jumping with joy I will draw attention to us. John held Grace's hand and said some day Grace, some day.

They turned and walked back along the beach, before they reached the crowded part they kissed, then continued their walk back to the car. In the car Grace said we should go to Cunningham's for fish and chips. When they got their fish and chips they drove out to Newtown cove and ate them there, then back to the coast road, through Fenor and on to Annestown, Boatstrand and parked at Kilmurrin cove, the tide was out full by now, so they walked out through the hole that was the entrance to the back strand, John turned to the left climbed on to the cliff that concealed the back strand from the main beach, then reached down and helped Grace up, a small inlet in the cliff about twenty feet long and five feet wide was an ideal swimming pool when the tide was out, the water was crystal clear.

Its beautiful here Grace said, peaceful and quiet, it's a shame we don't have our swimming togs. We could go skinning dipping John said. Oh I couldn't Grace said what if someone came. Well John said maybe you can't, but I can, John took of his clothes and jumped into the water. Grace stood up and looked around and said John, John come out someone might see. So John said, what have they to see, I have nothing different than they have. Grace laughed and said you're mad. Are you coming in John said. No I can't. Why not, John asked. I have never taking off my clothes in front of a man before. You won't have to John said I'll turn my back. No I can't. All right John said and swam towards the mouth of the inlet, he heard a splash and turned around.

Grace was in the water, he swam towards her, when they met they embraced and kissed, then swam out of the inlet and on to the sandy beach, and made love for the first time. They lay there together in silence arms entwined. Grace said, what are you thinking about. A poem John answered lying here with you in my arms it came to mind. Can I hear it?

Together

1

Here the land meets the sea, and so ends our walk
We will sit on the shoreline and there we will talk
About our future together and what it may hold
We will live for each for other and watch it unfold
Then a race towards the water and we will jump in
So happy together we will go for a swim
At one with nature, in the home of the fish
We'll touch each other, and tenderly kiss
When we emerge from the ocean, your hand in mine
We will lie on the sand and rest for a while

2

No clouds to be seen, blue skies high above
On a quiet beach in Ireland, we will make love
As we lay there together, our bodies entwined
We know the memory of this will last a lifetime
We will walk together life's unpredictable road
Sharing life's pleasure and sharing life's load
And when we are older we will think of our youth
Spent searching for pleasure, and seeking the truth
Tomorrow will come, but what will it bring
In the darkness of winter, we'll think of spring.

Oh John that's just what we have done, it's as if whoever wrote it knew what happened and wrote that poem about it, I will think of this day when winter comes, this winter, next winter, and every winter to come. We should be going Grace John said, Bridget will wonder where we've gone to, John kissed Grace, then they dressed and walked hand in hand back to the car, drove up the valley road and into the yard.

Bridget came out when she heard them coming, Charles has come down stairs she said. A look of sadness crossed Grace's face as if the very mention of his name put an end to her lovely day. John saw it and said. In the darkness of winter we'll think of spring. Grace looked at John smiled and said I must go now, and thanks for driving me to town and for, well for everything. It was a wonderful day Grace I hope we will repeat it soon. Grace answered I'm sure we will.

Haymaking Again

Monday morning it was make hay while the sun shines. Billy and John were piking hay, and also Grace and Bridget, Paddy Casey had come up to help, it was ten o'clock and Charles had not yet appeared. Fr Richard came in the lane he slowed as he passed lowered his window and said God bless the hard work, and then drove into the yard. Why is it Billy said that those who never have to work hard always say, God bless it.

John was watching Patsy raking the hay with some kind of contraption he had never seen before, it had two large iron wheels and was pulled by a horse, it had spikes at the front and back, the front spikes moved along the ground gathering the hay into a large bundle, when Patsy pulled a lever the front and back spikes reversed positions, and if Patsy wasn't careful as the back spikes tumbled over he could easily be injured. Patsy dispersed these mounds of hay around the field, then the haymakers turned them into cocks.

Fr Richard parked his car near the pump and walked into the kitchen, Charles was at the table drinking some tea.

You should be helping in the hayfield Richard said. I'm paying people to be there. Good God Charles even Grace and Bridget are helping, you know that hay must be saved as fast as it can before the rain come. There is no sign of rain Charles answered. Maybe not Richard said but you should be out there. I've told you I'm paying people to do it for me. If you keep carrying on this way you soon won't be able to pay anyone. I never wanted to come out here that was you and father's fault, I'm not a farmer, I'm a City man bred born and reared, and I should have stayed there with the girl I wanted to be with.

You have a great place here Charles, a lovely wife and home, what more do you want. Good God Richard you made a match for me with someone I never knew, all Grace and I are to you is an investment, a bloody investment, well you can take your investment and shove it. Charles pull yourself together, you're a grown man, put all that nonsense of love and living happily ever after behind you, whether you like it or not you are a married man now and that's the way you are going to stay, half the marriages in Ireland were arranged like yours, so get rid of the self pity, get out and get on with it. Charles went to the drinks cabinet and took out a bottle of whiskey. Richard said no Charles not at this time of day.

He took the bottle of Charles saying I'm going to the hay field to give a hand, I want to see you there in ten minutes, you have to run this farm and make it profitable, if you don't you won't get a penny from the family, you can't expect Grace to run this place on her own, what you need is a good day's work to sweat out all the alcohol you have consumed, God Charles if you're not careful you will end up in some institution getting dried out.

Richard joined them in the hayfield, Grace went over to him. Did you talk to him she asked, is he coming out. I spoke to him he'll be here soon. I hope so Grace said I can't run this place on my own, I was thinking of selling my share before she could continue. Richard said what, sell, sell, you can't do that you can't leave, where, would you go. As far away from here as possible, maybe to Dublin, I could get a job there. Nonsense Richard said anyway who would buy half a farm. Grace said, the people who own the other half that would give them full ownership, a good return on your investment, after all that's all I ever was an investment. Grace Richard said maybe it was an investment at the beginning, but you are part of our family now, I like you, father likes you. What about Charles, Grace asked. Charles will do what we tell him.

Richard do you not think that is the problem, he only married me because ye made him, I realise now he never wanted me, he was just obeying orders, he was, is in love with another woman, he should have been brave enough to say no to you and go with her, but he wasn't, I should have realised that marrying someone to hold onto a farm was very, very foolish. Grace, don't do anything you may regret. I have already done that by marrying Charles. Charles will pull himself together, everything will be alright I'm sure it will. Grace looked to where John was piking hay, and thought, Richard how can I tell you that I will regret marrying Charles for the rest of my life, and the only way my life will ever be all right is if I can spend it with John Grey.

They saw Charles come into the field, a pike on his shoulder, he started to cock some hay near Bridget and Billy, he worked busily for about half an hour the sweat poured down his face, the heat and drink were taking their toll, he took a hanky from his pocket and wiped his forehead. Bridget misjudged a pike of hay and it landed on Charles. He dropped his pike, brushed the hay away, the dust from the hay stuck to the sweat on his face, he was angry now, he turned to Bridget and said you stupid woman what do you think you're doing. I'm sorry Bridget said it was an accident. Accident, accident, Charles said I'll give you accident, Charles picked up his pike, he ran towards Bridget. Billy stuck out his leg, Charles tripped over it into a mound of hay.

Richard came over and said Charles what do you think you're doing have you gone completely mad, that is no way to behave over a bit of dust and hay. Charles got up he was shaking, he angrily stuck his pike in the ground and walked towards the house. Grace went over to Bridget are you all right she asked. I'm fine Bridget said, a bit shook up I'll be O K. Half an hour later they saw Charles drive out the lane and turn towards town. Grace said to Richard do you still think he will pull himself together. I have never seen him behave like that before Richard said. I have Grace answered.

What time is it, she asked Richard. It's twelve o clock he answered. Bridget and I are going in to make tea and sandwiches, come in around half twelve, Paddy, Patsy, and Billy are going to cycle home for dinner what about you John. Oh I'll go in and make myself something. Not at all Grace said come in with Richard and join us is that all right Richard she asked. Oh yes why not, after all he did drive me to town yesterday.

John and Richard were sitting at the table, Bridget poured the tea. Grace was standing behind Richard with the sandwiches. I was thinking about yesterday Richard said. John looked at Grace, so was I he said. About the, Richard looked at Bridget before he continued, about the bad apples in the barrel, I don't know where you heard it, but we have had a few complaints, but I don't think we can take them seriously, it's just people looking for attention, I don't think any Priest would do such things.

I think you should take the complaints seriously John answered if you don't it will do a lot of damage to the Church. Fr Richard said at the first opportunity we move them on. That won't solve it Father, that will only add to the problem, if a Priest is doing it in one parish he will do it in the next, people trust the Priests they look up to them, these people are betraying that trust, you should speak to the Bishop.

Bridget said what are ye talking about, surely you're not going to bother the Bishop about a few bad apples in a barrel, can't you get them out yourself before they rotten the whole barrel. John looked at Richard and said, that is exactly what they will do. Grace said that's enough talk, eat those sandwiches, we still have a lot of hay to save.

John and Richard were back in the hayfield at half one, Paddy, Patsy, and Billy joined them a few minutes later, Grace and Bridget came out at half two, Patsy continued to rake the hay into mounds, the cocks of hay were plentiful now. In the sweltering heat they would stop now and then for a drink of water from bottles that Grace and Bridget had brought from the pump. At about four o'clock Richard said to Grace I must be going now, I'll try and get out tomorrow. Thanks for the help Grace said. Richard answered it's the least I can do to make up for Charles absence. Richard picked up his coat and walked to the yard for his car. John went over to Grace and said he's not a bad haymaker.

Grace said they have a lot invested in this farm, if Charles don't shape up he'll be moved back to town, on the excuse he is needed in the shop, and a manager put in his place, this farm will have to show a profit, and when it suits them they will sell it. Will I see you this evening, John asked. I hope so Grace said, I'll be in the orchard at about eight meet me there.

John was walking across the yard at about five to eight. Bridget came out from the house, took her bike from the wall and said to John, where are you off to. Just out for an evening stroll Bridget, you seem to be in a hurry. I'm meeting Patsy she said, Grace is in the orchard. I might join her John said. I'm sure she could do with some company Bridget answered. John walked around by the end of the house and into the orchard.

Grace was sitting on a garden seat, the back door of the house was open John could hear music coming from a wireless inside the house. That's nice music he said to Grace. I was listening to radio eireann, a programme called ballad makers Saturday night, that's Joe Lynch singing the Cottage by the Lee.

John climbed over the seat and sat down beside her. I'm glad you came she said I've been sitting here thinking. About what, John asked. About the farm, the future, us, I was talking to father Richard today I told him I was considering selling my half of the farm. What John said, you can't do that, what would you do, where would you go. I don't know yet, maybe to Dublin. Grace this is your home, you love it here you never wanted to be anywhere else. That was before I met you John, you could come with me, we could be together for the rest of our lives, just you and I, no complications no Charles, I can't stay here, I just can't, locked in a loveless marriage, I know it's my fault, I should never have married Charles, I made a mistake, do I have to pay for it for the rest of my life.

It was a mistake by all concerned John said you never should have been put in that position, Father Richard, his father, your father they should have known better, good God what choice did they give you, marry Charles or put your father to the county home, don't put all the blame on yourself you did what you had to do at that time. What does it matter now John who's at fault I'm married now and it can't be undone, that's why we have to get away from here and start a new life elsewhere, you do want to be with me John.

Of course I do Grace more than anything in this world. It's just, well, when in Dublin or wherever if my memory came back who will I be. You'll still be yourself John, maybe a different name, maybe no longer John Grey, but John Grey is just a name, changing your name won't change you, you'll still look the same, feel same, the same mind, the same interests, and hopefully still love me. No matter who I am Grace I will always love you. Come on Grace said let's go for a walk out the lane, Grace and John walked hand in hand out the lane, it was a beautiful July evening, the Blackbird and Thrush were competing in song for attention, if a stranger met John and Grace that July evening, he would think they hadn't a care in the world, that they were just a young couple in love and the world was theirs and theirs alone, John started to recite a poem.

A Dream of Peace and Love

Summer evenings under a sky of blue,
I'll walk through shady lanes with you
We'll live in a dream like world, of happiness and Christmas bells
We'll watch our love unfurl, as we stroll through glistening dells
When winter days turn to spring, and evenings ever growing longer
We'll sit and listen to all birds sing, and know our love is growing stronger
We'll build our home on the clouds above, far away from man's self made grief
Live to our own ideals of love, not be dictated to by other men's belief
On our world, this war torn earth, men are striving to annihilate each other
But we'll find contentment by a glowing hearth, never lift a hand to kill a brother
If everyone could live together, accepting each other for what we are
Living in harmony all creeds and colour, no more hatred, no more war
The human race must change its way, if our dream of peace is to be kept alive
Living for peace living for love, that's the only way we can survive

That's unusual John, but the war is not long over, I can't see people rushing out to start another one. I have no doubt Grace that those who have to stop the bullets, or those who get blown to smithereens by the bombs, they won't start any wars, but the manipulators the power seekers, those who will never endanger themselves, watching from a safe distance at their men being slaughtered, urging them out of the trenches and up and over to oblivion, we are all just pawns in their game. John, don't spoil this lovely evening with talk of bombs and bullets. You're right Grace it's a lovely evening, let's enjoy it.

Grace said I'm going to talk to father Richard again they will just have to buy my half of the farm I can't stay here anymore.

Grace it's all right we're together now let's enjoy it, why spoil the present by worrying about the future. John I asked before why didn't you come to this valley before I met Charles, now I ask why did you come here at all, my life was uncomplicated everything I wanted was here, the farm, my horses, I could accept Charles for what he was, I lived my life, he lived his, then you walked in and turned the whole lot upside down. It happened Grace I came to the valley, we met, fell in love, now we have to decide if we want to live with love or without it, is it right that you should be condemned to a life of total unhappiness because two people made a match for you with a total stranger, I love you Grace, you say you love me, maybe I'm being selfish but right now nothing else matters. Grace faced John and said I do love you, standing there together in that lane on that July evening, as the sun was setting behind the Comeragh Mountains, and as they kissed, Grace thought, John was right nothing else in the world matters.

All day Tuesday the haymaking continued, Charles hadn't been seen since he left on Monday. It was Grace who had to carry on with John, Paddy, Billy, Patsy and Bridget, Billy went to bring the cows in at half four, Grace and Bridget went in at five, Grace to prepare something to eat, Bridget to milk the cows with Billy, John, Paddy, and Patsy worked on until half seven.

Patsy untackled the horses and said I think I'll take them in for water and food, they have done a good days work, Paddy said I think we'll all call it a day. John walked into the farmyard, went to the pump for a drink, then went upstairs to his room, he lit the stove with some timber from the workshop, put on the kettle and waited for it to boil, he poured the water into the basin then filled the kettle again and put it back on the stove for his tea, he washed and shaved, he was sitting at the table eating when he heard a crash in the yard, he went to the window and saw Charles car up against the water trough. Charles got out and staggered towards the door, he banged on the door and then slumped down on to the step, he shouted Grace, Grace, help me in. Grace opened the front door, and called Bridget and together they picked up Charles brought him to the kitchen and put him sitting on a chair at the table. Thanks Bridget Grace said. Will you be ok Bridget asked. Yes, yes Grace answered. I'll be in my room if you need me Bridget said.

Attempted Rape

Charles for God sake look at the state you're in, where have you been, you should be here saving the hay not drinking in town. To hell with the hay, Charles said and to hell with the farm too, all you ever think about is the farm, I don't give a dam about the farm, or you either, I never wanted to come out here, I was happy in town, I was living my life the way I wanted to live it, I was with the girl I wanted to be with, but they took it all away, took it all away and what did they give me in return a farm, a bloody farm, I'm not a farmer never was, and never will, you can do what you want with it.

Charles struggled up from the table went to the drinks cabinet and took out a bottle of whiskey. No Charles Grace said you've had enough, Grace tried to take the bottle of Charles, his voice was slurred as he said dammed right I've had enough, enough of you, enough of this place he pushed Grace against the table and hauled himself up the stairs.

As he passed Bridget's room her door was opened, he saw her sitting on her bed sewing a dress he staggered into the room. Bridget he said have a drink with me, the wife tells me I've had enough, what do you, think. No. no Charles Bridget said I don't drink. Come on Charles said just one, No Charles, no. No Charles said, no, that seems to be the favourite word of the women in this house, I'm not taking no for an answer, you're going to drink with me whether you like it or not. Bridget got off the bed and ran towards the door. Charles caught her arm as she passed and pushed her back on the bed. Grace, Grace Bridget shouted. Charles went to the door and bolted it, saying, it's time you and I had a bit of fun.

Grace ran up the stairs and tried to open the door. Charles, Charles she shouted open this door, she banged on the door and tried to push it open, Charles, Charles don't do anything stupid, Grace ran down the stairs and across the yard to John she shouted come quick. What wrong, John asked. It's Charles, he's drunk and he's locked himself in Bridget's room, God knows what he's going to do, he's crazy with whiskey. John ran across the yard and up the stairs, opened the door he shouted or I'll break it down, John stepped back on the landing then charged the door with his shoulder, the bolt gave way and John was in the room.

He saw Bridget struggling with Charles on the bed he caught Charles by the shoulder and flung him across the room. Charles struggled to his knees and then stood up. Ah he said the poetic John Grey, the handy man, let's see if you are as good with your fists as you are with words. I don't want to fight you John said, you're drunk. We'll see who's drunk Charles said swinging at John. John stepped swiftly aside, Charles fell on his face on the floor. John picked him up and brought him to his room laid him on his bed, then went back to Grace and Bridget, Bridget was crying. Grace was trying to console her. Did anything happen, did he do anything to you she asked. No Bridget said God if John hadn't broken the door down, what would have happened. Don't think about it Grace said come down stairs I'll make you a cup of tea, as John walked out the door to the landing, Charles was coming towards him with his shotgun. Charles John said now don't be foolish, everything is all right, no one got hurt, don't make matters worse.

You all had a good laugh at me in the hayfield, Charles said, now we'll see who'll have the last laugh. Put the gun down Charles John said again. No Charles said now lock Bridget in my room then I'll lock you, and my so called wife out of the way in her room. John could see the sweat run down Charles face, he was trembling and out of control, John thought he's capable of doing anything,

John said let's talk out here. No Charles said lock Bridget in the room I have unfinished business with her. John locked Bridget in the room. Now Charles said the two of you in Grace's room. Grace and John walked towards the door Grace went in, John stood in the doorway, Charles shoved the barrel of the gun into John's back, inside he said. John swung around hitting the barrel of the gun with one hand and pushed Charles hard with the other, Charles staggered back against the banister, broke it and fell to the floor, John heard the gun go off he ran down the stairs. Charles was lying on his back. John knelt down beside him. I've shot myself, I've bloody shot myself in the knee. John said have you got any twine, get me some twine, or one of Charles ties, Grace ran to his bedroom and came back with a tie, John wrapped the tie around Charles thigh and pulled it tight. Grace went and let Bridget out of the room, and got a pillow and a blanket from her bed, and brought them down to John.

John put the pillow under Charles head, John said to Grace wrap the blanket around him and keep him warm, where's the keys of the car. They're probably in it Grace answered. I'm going for Doctor Walsh John said. Tell him to phone Fr Richard Grace said. When Charles hit the water trough he broke one of the lights, otherwise the car was alright John sat in, reversed the car away from the trough and drove as fast as he could to Doctor Walsh's. He ran from the car, knocked on the door, the door was opened by the Doctor, who recognised John and said John Grey the poetry man, how's the memory. Still the same John answered can you come quick Doctor, an accident at Arscott's.

What happened the Doctor asked. Charles accidently shot himself. I'll get my bag the Doctor said. You had better call an ambulance John said it looks bad, and Grace said could you please call Fr Richard. My wife Una will do that for me while I'm driving down. John let Doctor Walsh go first then drove behind him back to the farm

Grace and Bridget were still with Charles when they got there. Doctor Walsh knelt down beside Charles and looked at the knee he took a scissors from his bag and cut the leg of Charles trousers. My God he said that's bad, I'll give him an injection it will stabilise him until the ambulance come, who tied the tie around his thigh the Doctor asked. John did Grace answered. The Doctor looked at John. You did well, where did you learn that. I don't know Doctor I just knew it had to be done. You probably saved him from bleeding to death, there's nothing much can be done until he gets to hospital.

Forty minutes later the ambulance drove in the yard, it was leaving with Charles when Fr Richard arrived. What happened, how is he, he asked. Not too good Doctor Walsh answered, I'll follow the ambulance. I'll come to Fr Richard said, the Doctor answered he will go straight to the operating theatre come in later I'll know something by then.

Fr Richard looked at the gun and blood on the floor he saw the blood on John's hands and clothes he looked up at the banister, in God's name he said what happened here, Bridget ran to her room crying. Grace said come to the Kitchen I'll make some tea, you come too John. Fr Richard said will someone please tell me what happened here, my brother's gone to hospital in a very critical condition, right now we don't if he will survive, he was shot, I need to know what happened, someone has a lot of explaining to do, this is serious, I think I'll ask Bridget to go for the guards. John said it is more serious for Charles than you think, and Bridget is too shocked to go for the guards, I'll tell you what happened and if you still want to call the guards I'll go for them myself, John told Richard exactly what happened, from the time Grace called him to when he came back with the doctor, when he finished he said to Fr Richard do you still want me to go for the guards, I'm sure they will charge him with attempted rape, and attempted murder.

My God Grace Richard said I'm sorry, how could he, I never thought he would go this far, what got into him are you alright, is Bridget alright, he went into the hall and called Bridget down, I'm sorry Bridget he said did he hurt you. Oh Father what would have happened if John wasn't here. I'll go for the guards John said. No, no Richard answered it will ruin my Father, it, it will, he broke off and said no more.

Ruin you as well John said, that would be some bit of justice John continued, after ye ruined Charles's life by sending him out here. We could never foresee this happening he said. I'm sure you couldn't John answered, but it has happened and the question is now, what are you going to do about it. What do you mean Richard asked. John asked Grace, do you want to call the guards. Grace answered if you and Bridget want to I think you should. No, no Richard said you can't. Richard Grace said Bridget has every right to call the guards she was attacked by a drunken lunatic. John had a shotgun against his back. I know Richard said, but not the Guards surely we can come to some arrangement. It wouldn't look well in court John said, a Priest's brother and a gentleman farmer to boot, charged with attempted murder, and attempted rape of a servant girl, those things don't happen in holy Ireland. Fr Richard looked at John and said I'll see that Bridget will get a substantial financial award and you John what do you want.

Justice John answered. Fr Richard said Bridget has gone through enough we don't want her to go through the ordeal of guard's and court, what good will it do her if Charles is taken to court, as I said we will compensate her well. It's a pity you weren't as concerned about Charles welfare in the past as you are now, but I think it's up to Bridget the decision is hers. No, no Bridget said I couldn't, I don't want to go to court everyone staring at me no, no. It's all right Grace said, you don't have to go. We'll report it as an accidental shooting

John said. Now Richard said I must go to the hospital, Grace, will, you come with me.

No Grace said I'm not going to see him ever again. But he is your husband he needs you now. Why should he need me now when he never needed me, and even if he does need me, I don't need him, not now, not ever again, John will drive me to your father's house in the morning, you be there, you can tell me how he is, and we can discuss the future of this place. But, Grace. No buts Richard that's what I want. Are, you sure. I was never so sure of anything in my life.

At eight o' clock the following morning John went into the cow house, Billy and Patsy were there milking, John said I won't be in the hayfield until this afternoon, I must drive Grace to town, Charles had an accident last night. I saw the damage to the car Patsy said. No not in the car Patsy, with a shotgun, he accidently shot himself in the knee. Is it bad Billy asked. It is John answered anyway I'll be back as soon as I can, I must get something to eat now I'll see you later, John was ready to go at ten o'clock,

Grace and Bridget came out, are you alright Bridget John asked. I'm grand Bridget answered, what did you tell Patsy. I just said Charles had an accident. I think that's for the best Bridget said, Patsy is hot headed God knows what he might do if he knew. John opened the door for Grace and they drove out the lane. I mentioned the other day John about selling my share of the farm and going to Dublin, what happened last night convinced me it's the right thing to do, will you come with me.

You know I will Grace, but this is your home, where you always wanted to be, are you sure. Yes I am, Dublin, London, anywhere, a new beginning, a new life with you. As they got near the city, Grace said I'll direct you to where Charles Mother and Father live, take the next right, then left it's the end house on the right. John stopped the car Grace got out and walked up the path. Richard saw her coming and opened the door Mother and Father are not here he said they are at the hospital.

How is he Grace asked, not too good they had to amputate, and there's a bone broke in his back, I'm afraid his working days on the farm are over. His working days on the farm never started Grace said if he had been helping with the hay instead of drinking this would never have happened. Maybe not, Richard said, with hindsight maybe we should never have made a match with you. Match or no match Grace said it was no excuse for what he did last night.

Will you have some tea Richard asked. No thanks, John drove me in, Patsy and Billy are at the hay, we've got to get back and get on with it, Charles cannot come to the house while I'm there, not after last night and what he tried to do to Bridget, I spoke to you the other day about selling my share of the farm, that's what I want to do.

That won't be easy Richard said not many people want to by half a farm. I was hoping Grace said the person who own the other half, might buy it, your Father. I don't think Father would be interested the only reason he invested was to try and get Charles to settle down. Well Grace said that leaves only one option. What's that Richard asked. Sell the whole farm Grace answered.

What Richard said, sell the whole farm we can't do that. Grace said, as long as I'm at the farm Charles is not coming near the place, if you or your father insist on him coming back, I'll go to the Guards and tell them everything, and get a barring order against him, so if you don't want your brother charged with attempted rape, attempted murder, and wife battering it would be in your interest to persuade your Father to sell.

Fr Richard said wife battering Grace what do you mean. Grace answered on our wedding night he got drunk and hit me. God Grace

I'm sorry about all this Fr Richard said, if there is anything I can do. Grace interrupted him and said, get your father to sell, that's all you need to do, the farm is in good shape now, the hay will be saved, so will the corn, you will get a lot more than you paid for it, whoever buys it, will have time to decide what crops they want next year. I suppose Richard said under the circumstances it's the only thing to do, all right he said we'll sell and share fifty, fifty. No grace said your Father put a lot of money into it, but not as much as half of the farm, sixty per cent for me and forty for your father. Richard said I'll talk to our Solicitors.

Will you go to see Charles. No Grace answered. What will Father and Mother think. Tell them the truth Richard, tell them that we should never have married and that he should have been left in town with the woman he wanted to be with, one more thing I'm going to try and get a job in Dublin. It won't be easy to get a position Richard said. You forget Grace said my Brother in law is a Priest, who is friends with the Bishop, and I'm sure the Bishop here, know the Bishop in Dublin, as always in Ireland it's not what you know but who you know, now I must go, as Grace walked towards the door. Fr Richard said have you always known what you wanted from life. No Richard Grace answered, not always but I know now.

Within two weeks the hay was saved and in the shed. Fr Richard drove out one day and told Grace that Charles was getting better and that his Father had agreed to sell the Farm, a date was not yet set for the auction, he would contact her with the date later on. Grace said I'm glad Charles is getting better. Better but very unhappy Richard said, confined to a wheelchair can't be easy, he's lost his leg, lost you. He never had me to lose Grace answered. Anyway that's how the situation is Richard said, I'll call out again soon, look after the farm and let's hope we get a good price for it. Don't worry Richard it's in good hands, does your Mother and Father know what happened here.

Yes I told them, Father is as mad as hell with Charles and very disappointed, Mother won't talk to either of us, she blames us for everything. And so she should Grace said and me as well. You're young Grace, us older adults should have known better, anyway what's done is done, regret and recrimination won't repair or undo the past, we must move on. Unfortunately Grace said in the eyes of the Church I can't move on, or undo the marriage either, as far as the Church is concerned Charles and I must stay together as long as we are alive. I must be going now I'll see you in a few weeks. Yes all right Grace said call out anytime.

Harvest

It was a few days before the fifteenth of August, a Church holiday and the race meeting in Tramore, the most important day of the year in Waterford. Patsy and Billy were all talk about it, they had been saving their money for weeks, from early morning motor cars, horse and traps, bicycles, people walking, all forms of transport would be strung out along the roads that led to Tramoe, trains out from Waterford City would be packed. Some would go to the race meeting, but the majority would throng the pubs, dancehalls, amusements arcades, fish and chip shops, and for one day in the year they would put behind them the harsh reality of life, and drink, sing, and dance all day and for most of the night. So Tramore was the topic of conversation in the farmyard on that August morning, as Patsy took the reaper and binder out of the shed, and asked John to repair the lats on the canvas.

John was looking in amazement at the machine when Grace joined them, never saw anything like it John said what's it for. What's it for Grace said, it's for cutting and binding the corn. How does it work John asked. Grace explained do you see that blade standing up at the side, that will be lowered down and when the horses pull the machine, the wheels will move the blade, the blade will cut the corn, the corn will fall on to the canvas with the lats, and it will be conveyed up to the binder, a ball of twine will be placed here, Grace put her hand where the twine would be, the corn will pass through it, it will be tied into bundles and flicked on to the ground, then you, Billy and I will gather them up and stand four of them against each other and make a stook.

A what, John said. A stook Billy shouted, when the four bundles stand against each other it's called a stook, sure everyone know what a stook is, and then after a few days we will have to gather all the stooks together and make stacks, and then we will load all the stacks on to the horses carts and bring them to the haggard and make a rick, to keep it dry until the thresher come. That will take a lot of time and work John said. It will, Patsy said, but we'll get there, now do you see those damaged lats, unless you replace them we won't get anything done. All right John said I'll get on with it. What are you and Billy doing Patsy Grace asked. We're going to put edge on the scythes and start clearing the headlands if the weather lasts we'll cut next week.

Everyone was up early on the fifteenth of August, the cows were brought in early, Patsy and Billy milked them, John tried to help, but wasn't so successful, that was the only work that was done that day, almost everyone in the parish went to mass, and from about ten o'clock onwards crowds of people were on their way to Tramore, on foot, on bikes, in motor cars and horse and traps. Those who could afford it hired the only two hackney cars that were in the parish, owned by Andy Tibbs and Paddy Whelan. Andy and Paddy would make several trips to Tramore, all day and well into the night. Are you going to the races, John asked Grace. I don't think so she answered. Good John said we have the day to ourselves, how should we spend it. I'll pack a picnic basket, we'll go to the cove have a swim and relax. Sounds good to me John said.

At half two Grace and John were relaxing on the beach which was deserted apart from themselves everyone having gone to Tramore, have you any regrets John asked now that the decision has been made to sell the farm. No John I'm looking forward to our life in Dublin together, no more secrecy, we can walk down the street holding hands, no one will take a bit of notice, you and I together, come on John said let's take a dip, when they came in they lay down together on the sand, what if someone see us. Right now Grace answered I don't care, they kissed two people on a deserted beach in love. John said the other day when we were talking about the reaper and binder. What about it Grace asked. Billy mentioned a thresher.

That's right Grace said when all the corn is saved and brought to the haggard the thresher will come to thresh the corn, did you ever see a thresher. I don't think so Grace but a poem came to my mind about a steam engine and thresher. That would be right John the steam engine would work the thresher, the same as the stone breaker you saw in the Quarry can I hear the poem. Sure Grace why not.

Steam Engine

1

She moved towards the village in a cloud of smoke and steam
My children could not believe it, what is this strange machine
They stood and gazed in wonder, a sight they never saw before
This lovely old steam engine going slowly past our door
And with it came fond memories to those of us that's older
As I stood and watched with my child upon my shoulder

2

This lovely old steam engine, a survivor from the past
She had her days of glory when this world didn't go so fast
In the days before the combine and the modern silorater
She would go from farm to farm with thresher and elevator
She would travel through the country, steam over hill and vale
Sharing the roads of Ireland with the Donkey and Clydesdale

3

A tell tale plume of smoke, a yell she's on her way
That farmyard would buzz on those far off threshing days

They would shovel in the coal and really build up steam
All would work as one, man, thresher and machine
From dawn till dusk they would give their all
As one rick got large and the other one small

4

The children laughed as they played about
Thirsts were quenched with pints of stout
They would bank her down for the hours of night
Then up, and off again at dawn's first light
Stoke her up and then be on their way
Another threshing, another farm, another day

5

The smell of burning coal is in the air
That old machine stands graceful there
With the help of skilful hands she will survive
To serve as a bridge across the gap of time
Brought from the past to be with us here
For all of us, a chance to view yesteryear

John that's the strangest poem I've heard from you yet, you talk of the steam engine as if it didn't exist anymore, brought from the past, it's not brought from the past, it's with us here and now, and what in God's name is a silorator. I don't know Grace, I don't know where that or any of the poems came from.

I've read in the papers John about something called a combined harvester, some kind of a machine they have in America, and in some parts of this country it's a cross between a reaper and binder and a thresher, and at the start of the poem, the children gazed in wonder at a sight they never saw before, a child would have to be from another world not to have seen a steam engine, and a bridge across the gap of time, a bridge to where, to what.

John where are you from, where are these poems from, I'm afraid John, afraid of losing you, afraid you'll vanish out of this valley as mysteriously as you came in. John held Grace, don't be afraid he said, I'm here with you, we're together, we're going to Dublin together, just you and I Grace.

The days were still warm and dry but the evenings were a bit chilly, John had a good fire in the stove, and when Bridget cycled off to meet Patsy, Grace would cross the yard to John's room, there they would sit together talking, reading, very happy in each other's company. On one such occasion Grace was sitting on the floor, her back against John's bed, a book on her lap, John was at the table carving a small piece of wood.

What are you making, Grace asked. It's for you John answered, but you can't see it until it's finished, you're very interested in that book what's it about. It's the one I gave you, the poems of John Keats Grace answered. For one who died so young he wrote some lovely poems John said. So sad Grace said, can you imagine what his feelings were, leaving his home in Hampstead, brought to Italy to die, leaving the love of his life behind, what would he have wrote if he knew he was never going to see her again. I don't know, John said, maybe he was too sick to write at that stage.

Maybe John, but if he could, if it was possible for him to write one more time under the plum tree in the garden what would he have wrote. Gosh Grace John said, I don't know, who knows what would be in the mind of a poet like him. If you had to leave me in the morning John, what would you, write. What would I, write. I don't know Grace the thought of leaving you never entered my mind. Grace smiled and started to read her book again.

John got up from the table, searched a drawer in the press for a pen and note book, he began to write, crossed of what he had written, and began again, he did this a few times until he was satisfied with what he had, he went and sat beside Grace on the floor and said you asked what I would write if we had to part well this is it.

I sit here and peace is mine, my heart is happy and so contented, just to sit, to dream, to be happy, all I ask is to be with you forever / to cherish and to love you, and you to love me, to hold your hand, to share my life with you, to leave you never

I must leave here and all this happiness will stay, but I will take with me a memory of you, and of this happy time, of your smile, your face. Tomorrow and forever I will think of you and remember how we laughed and loved in this time and place.
All things are planned for us, we plan nothing for ourselves.

Oh John, don't, don't talk of leaving, the thought of it bring shivers down my spine. Grace you asked what I would write. I know but don't, don't ever again. I'm sorry Grace, come here, John and grace hugged, and they made love on the floor.

It was a Saturday in early September John was standing in the headland of the cornfield, watching Patsy complete the first circle on the reaper and binder, he was amazed by the machine, the way it worked, and how neatly it tied the bundle, he picked up a bundle and stood there examining it. Billy said are you going to stand there all day with that bundle or are you going to pick up a few more and stand them against each other. I never saw anything like it before Billy, it amazes me. It must be a backward part of the country you came from John, I thought the day of the scythe was gone, and all farmers had a reaper and binder by now.

The work continued steady all morning Patsy circling the field, as the standing corn was cut by the reaper, the bundles got more plentiful, they were gathered by Grace, Bridget, John and Billy, they worked in pairs Grace and John, Bridget and Billy at twelve o'clock Grace called Bridget and said we'll go in and make something to eat, John and Billy continued stooking until at around one o' clock, then they saw Grace and Bridget return with the tea and sandwiches.

They all sat down to rest and eat, Grace sat beside John, is there any news from town he asked. No not yet John, I thought Fr Richard might have called by now, they were interrupted by a shout from the road, Grace got up and saw Jeff Flynn the postman, she went over to the road and said hello to Jeff, Jeff handed her a letter and said I see you're all busy at the harvest, we are Grace said. Is that the mysterious John Grey I see, Jeff asked. Grace said, why, did you call him that.

Oh not just me Mrs, that's what they all call him, though I don't blame them, he is a bit of a mystery, not knowing who he is, or where he came from, he could have dropped out of the sky for all we know, anyway Mrs I must keep going. Good bye Jeff Grace said and returned to the field, Grace sat down beside John, opened and read the letter, it's from Fr Richard, Charles is out of hospital and recuperating in a convalescent home in Waterford, the sale of the farm is arranged for the end of October, when Grace finished reading the letter John said. So that's it then the date is set. Yes Grace said you and I can be settled in Dublin by Christmas.

Grace and Bridget gathered up the mugs and teapot and put them in the car, Patsy sat up on the reaper and binder and continued cutting, the stooking was progressing well, it was well into the afternoon when John straightened up to stretch his back, he was looking at the reaper and binder when suddenly another poem came to his mind.

Half An Autumn's Morn

1

I stood and watched the combine move through that field of corn
It cut and threshed that field of oats in half an autumn's morn
I watched the tractor move in close, the ripened grain to take
I listened but alas in vain, to hear the corncrake
To my mind then came a vision of that field of long ago
And all the work that it would take, that field of oats to grow
Two horses, man, one sod plough, turned that field from green to brown
Go on, keep off, come in!" words you'd hear as the seagulls circled round
And then would come the harrow and that would keep you fit
All day long you walked behind, as the horses chomped the bit
Manure and then the sower, and half the work was done
Then you prayed for April showers, followed by summer sun

2

Coming across the valley, carried on a gentle breeze
The sound of the reaper and binder circling the field
As the standing corn got smaller, of the bundles they were more
They were gathered by the workmen into stooks of four
From stooks they would make stacks, that was a special skill
As a youth I learned to make them, I could make them still
Once more they'd tackle horses, this time to haul a cart
To bring the corn to the haggard, and on the rick they'd start
When they had it finished, sure they'd feel very proud
You would see them walk around it, and survey it from the ground
Soon would come the thresher, and give two days threshing corn
But now they cut and thresh in half an autumn's morn.

John stood motionless looking across the field at the reaper and binder, but now it wasn't the reaper and binder he saw, but a large yellow machine, a man sitting in a cab high up in front, the machine was gobbling up the corn and spewing it out the back, Grace was watching John, she went over to him. John, John are you alright, you seem to be in a different world.

Can you see it Grace. Can I see what, Grace asked. The machine Grace the huge yellow machine. Where, John. John put his hands to his eyes and rubbed them, when he looked again the machine was gone the reaper and binder was still circling the field. I'm all right Grace, a vision, some sort of vision, it's gone now. Grace he asked could this field of corn be cut and threshed in half an autumn's morn.

You must be joking John, that would be impossible, we've got to cut, stook, and stack this field, then draw it to the haggard, and it will take at least a day and a half to thresh it, no hope of doing it in what did you say, half an autumn's morn, where did you get that idea. A poem grace, about some machine called a combined, cutting corn, and a tractor drawing it away, I don't know where these thoughts and visions are coming from, let's forget it for now Grace and get on with this stooking.

Grace and John continued with the work in silence for awhile then Grace said. John do you think what you saw today has something to do with your past. I don't know Grace, maybe, a big machine Grace, with a reel on it, something like the one on the reaper and binder, only ten times as big and on the front, not at the side, it cut the corn as it drove and the straw came out the back in rows along the field, I remember Grace you mentioning something in the paper about some machine in America, a kind of a cross between a reaper and binder and a threshing machine.

That's right John but where would you have seen one of them, were you ever in America. Not that I know of Grace, but these visions are becoming more frequent. Maybe Grace said, your mind, your memory, maybe it's a sign your memory is about to return. I hope so Grace. I'm frightened Grace said, when it comes back, who will you be, where will you have came from, will you go back there, and if you do will I be able to go with you, will you still love me.

Grace it will make no difference who I am, or where I came from, and where ever I'm going, I will always love you, today, tomorrow, and as long as I am capable of loving, I will love no one but you, now come here to me. Patsy will see us. I don't care Grace, right now I don't care if the whole world see us, you look beautiful with that piece of straw hanging from your hair, the sun shining on your face, how could anyone resist kissing you, even the bird's are queuing up to do so.

Bridget and Billy went to bring in the cows for milking at about four o' clock, Grace and John continued until Patsy stopped cutting at about five thirty and brought in the horses for food and water, Grace and John walked hand in hand behind him in the lane, Bridget and Billy were still milking when they reached the yard. I'll make something to eat, will you join me John. I think I'll go for a swim, harvesting is dusty work, I'll eat later, take the car Grace said, I must exercise my horse, I'll ride to the cove and meet you there.

A Mystery

John was at the cove at six o' clock, he lay down on a grassy bank in the sun and closed his eyes, when he heard the sound of a trotting horse he opened his eyes and saw Grace approaching. She brought the horse to a halt, dismounted and sat beside John. It's beautiful here John she said. It was until you came, now its beauty has faded in comparison to you. Grace had a quick look around then kissed John.

They stayed sitting and talking together until around seven o' clock, then Grace said I better take the horse home, I'll go for a quick swim John said. Will I see you later, Grace asked. Try and keep me away John answered. Grace mounted her horse and trotted up the valley road, she met Bridget and Patsy on the way to the cove. Is John still over there Patsy shouted as he passed. He is Grace said, he's going swimming, when they reached the cove, John was standing at the water edge.

Patsy shouted and waved. John waved back and said, I'll only be a few minutes. Bridget and Patsy sat on the grass and watched as John entered the water, when he was waist high he dived into a wave. Patsy and Bridget were watching for him to surface, after a few minutes Patsy stood up, I know he's a god swimmer he said, but he should have surfaced by now, he ran to the water edge. John, John he shouted where are you, he ran into the water where he last saw John, he searched around but to no avail.

Maybe he swam under water to the back strand Bridget said. Patsy ran up the cliff and climbed down to the back strand he shouted, and searched around, but John was nowhere to be seen, he went back to Bridget. Any sign of him she said. Not a sign he said, get on your bike Bridget and cycle as fast as you can to get Grace.

As she passed the Forge she shouted to Paddy Casey, John's in trouble at the cove, Paddy grabbed his bike and took off fast. When Bridget entered the farmyard Grace was watering the horse, the saddle still on. Grace, Grace she shouted John's in trouble in the water at the cove. Grace swung on to the horse and rode as fast as she could to the cove, when she got there Paddy and Patsy were in the water searching. What happened Patsy, she asked. He was standing in about three feet of water he dived into a wave, I haven't seen him since. Grace ran to her car, John had left the keys in it she drove to Kill village and over to the Garda barracks.

Guard Donlon was on duty, Grace explained what had happened. I'll contact Dunmore Gardie, they'll get out the life boat. Grace drove back to the cove, some locals had joined the search, the lifeboat arrived around eight thirty, they searched for about an hour then it got too dark, we'll resume at day break they said.

At first light the following morning Grace was on the shore, she was joined by many locals. Jamesie Murray organised the fishing boats from Boatsrand, they all joined the search. Coves, inlets caves, everywhere it was possible to search, was searched for about a week but all in vain, then the search was called off, everyone accepted now that John Grey would not be found, everyone except Grace.

She continued searching the shore, she would walk the cliff's and gaze out to sea, she spent a lot of time sitting by the inlet where she and John went skinny dipping, at night she would sit indoors, Bridget stayed with her most evenings, very few neighbours called, why should they, they didn't know Grace was grieving, to them John Grey was just one of Grace's workmen who had mysteriously appeared in the valley a few months ago, and now had just as mysteriously vanished. Patsy and Billy, with the help from neighbours finished cutting the corn, and it was brought to the haggard to await the thresher.

Patsy often called to the Forge to Paddy and they would talk about John, they couldn't understand how such a good swimmer could disappear in three feet of water.   It just didn't make sense Patsy said, I saw him standing there in the water, up to his waist is all he was, then he dived and just vanished, he could swim to Boatstrand and back, and to think he disappeared in three feet of water, Christ I can't understand it. It is strange Patsy, I can't believe he's gone he will be missed, but remember we don't know how John came to this valley, or where he came from, he seemed to have materialised out of the air, I suppose his coming here is a mystery and now his going is a mystery.

Where's Bridget. Keeping Grace company, Patsy answered, she's taking it bad, she and John were very close. I know, Patsy I know, ah come on we'll go to the village for a few pints it will take our mind of it. We may as well, Patsy answered I don't think I'll see Bridget this evening. How are the two of you getting on, Paddy asked. Good Paddy, good, I could be looking for a best man before the year is out. Glad to hear Paddy said, now come on let's go for a few bottles.

Loss

One Sunday about three weeks after John disappeared, Grace was walking to her car after Mass when she heard someone calling she turned around and saw Taigh O' Brien coming toward her. Mrs Arscott could you spare a few minutes I'd like to talk to you. About what, Grace asked. About John Grey he answered, but first how is Mr Arscott. Getting better Grace said. I suppose he'll be back on the farm soon. No Grace answered he won't be able to do farm work anymore, we are going to sell. John Grey is a big loss to you. You'll never know how much of a loss he is.

Grace about John, the last time we had a few drinks together, he gave me a poem he wanted my opinion on, I haven't it on me now, but I'd like you to have it, could I call down to you with it some evening. Of course Taigh, any evening this week I'll be there, Grace said good bye to Taigh and went to her car, on her way home she was wondering what was in the poem, she said out loud, John, John, oh how I miss you, why, why did you go, where did you go, all our plans John, Dublin, you and I together, gone, all gone, Oh my God, why, why.

Monday evening about four o 'clock Taigh drove into Grace's farm yard, went to the door and knocked. Bridget opened the door. Good evening Bridget is Mrs Arscott in Taigh asked. I'm sorry Bridget said she's not here at the moment. When will she be back. I don't know. Will you tell her I called. I will, is it important. It could be Taigh said. If you drive to Kilmurrin you should find her there. Thanks Bridget. Taigh parked his car beside Grace's and walked down the beach, he couldn't see her anywhere, the tide was out, he decided to go out the back strand, Grace was nowhere to be seen. He shouted Mrs Arscott, Mrs Arscott. Grace was standing on a rock near the edge of the cliff,

I'm up here she said. Taigh climbed up. My God Mrs Arscott he said this place is dangerous be careful you don't fall. She said I'll be careful Taigh, I have every reason to be.

Taigh said, Grace about John. What about him. We used to talk in the pub about poetry, about time travel. Time travel Taigh, surely that's impossible. Impossible Grace, maybe, but some lines in John's poems, Grace I'm a teacher and yet I never heard them before, I contacted some of my fellow teacher's around various parts of the country they never heard of them, you never heard of them. God I'm not making much sense am I, I think John's poems were written in the future by someone looking back on the past, and the past he was looking back at is our present.

He said in the pub one night is it yesterday, today, or tomorrow, were we here before, are we here now, will we be here again, maybe I'm making a fool of myself but do you think John Grey, was, is the kind of man that gets lost in three feet of water. Grace remembered the poem John recited the evening they went swimming together in the nude, she remembered what she said about it, it's as if whoever wrote it knew what happened, and wrote about it, thinking of that evening Grace had to fight the tears from her eyes before she said to Taigh, John is gone that is all that matters and I'll, we'll never see him again.

Gone yes Taigh said but not dead. Dead or gone Grace said, he is not here is he. No not here Grace, but he is someplace in the land of the living. But where is that someplace Taigh, can we go there, can we see him, talk to him, he is gone from here Taigh, and that's all that matters to me. John's poems grace, I've contacted poetry experts at some of the universities, they know their poetry and yet they never heard of any John's poems. You said John gave you a poem. He did Taigh said and reached into his pocket took out a piece of paper and handed it to Grace saying, I don't know if it's a poem or a prayer. Grace unfolded the paper and read.

Free Spirit

Do not look for me in a quiet Graveyard, for I am not within
When the leaves rustle on the trees, that is me
I am the wind on the high mountain, the laughing brook in the green valley
And I am also the sea spray on you face
Do not grieve for me, rejoice, for I am free
I have shaken off the shackles of my earthly existence
I can be what I want and travel at will
I will surf the cornfields in summer,
and in winter dance with the northern lights
I am the wisp of white clouds that float over the flowers of spring
And I drift with the autumn mist
Sometime in the future you too will cease your earthly existence
Then you will join with me, and together forever,
we will travel the never ending universe.

Grace finished the poem and was looking out to sea in silence. Taigh said, what, do you think. Grace answered I don't know what to think. Taigh said I think it's a poem about time travel, it says I can be what I want and travel at will. I don't think so Grace said, it mentions the end of earthly existence I think it's the soul or the spirit being set free after death. I still think it's time travel Taigh said, and John Grey has not departed this world, he is out there, somewhere, keep the poem I must go now. I'll walk back to the car with you Grace said, and thanks for the poem, and for, well talking about John, and if you are right maybe someday, someone will see him again, it's, it's been a sad time, no one knew how I felt about John, I, I couldn't tell anyone. Did you tell John, Taigh asked. Yes every chance I got. I understand, Taigh said, he was, is different. Yes Grace answered he certainly was.

Threshing

The good weather continued, Billy and Patsy were watching the thresher come in the lane, but where was the steam engine, the thresher was being pulled by a tractor, with the name fordson written on it. Patsy said to the driver, where's the steam engine. The days of the steam engine are in the past the driver answered, he tapped his hand on the tractor this is the future. But Billy said look at it, it's so small compared to a steam engine. Small but powerful the driver said. Patsy and Billy helped the driver to maneuver the thresher into position beside the rick, then they got a pick and shovel and levelled the ground for the wheels, and put timber blocks at each side of them to make sure it would not move when it was threshing. The driver said that should do it, all ready for the morning.

Grace and Bridget were in the kitchen, are you meeting Patsy tonight Grace asked. I am Bridget said, but I won't if you want me to stay with you. I'll be alright Bridget you go. I'm only going down to Paddy and Kathleen for a few hands of cards. Bridget went out at nine o' clock. Grace sat by the fire, she was thinking of the first day John walked in the yard, and the Sunday they went to Annestown, and their swims at their secret inlet, her thoughts were interrupted by a loud knock on the door, when she went to open it, Guard Donlon was standing there. Good night Mam he said. Good night Guard Grace answered. I'm sorry to bother you at this time of night, but there's been a development.

What do you mean Guard Grace asked. Some fishermen have taken a body from the sea down the coast. All feeling left Grace, she thought she was going to faint, she put her hand on the frame of the door to steady herself. Won't, won't you come in she said to the

Guard. The Guard followed grace in. Do you mind if I sit down Grace said. I think you should the Guard answered, I'll get you some water, he handed Grace the water and said are you better. Yes, yes Grace answered I'm alright, how may I help you. As I was saying, a man's body has been taken from the sea, could you, go to the morgue in the morning to identify him. The young man that's missing, he worked for you, you knew him well. I did, yes I did. The Garda car will call for you, I'll let myself out now good night, and I think you should get a good night's sleep you look a bit, well a bit drained. Guard, Grace said would you call to Paddy's Casey's on the way down and ask Bridget to come up. I'm going in there anyway Mam, for a game of cards I'm of duty now, I'll tell her. Grace went to the door with the Guard he took his bike from against the wall and said Good night again Mam.

Grace closed the door and sat down at the table, her hands were trembling she lay her head down on the table and said John, John, why, why, where, where did you go, are you somewhere in the land of the living as Taigh thinks or is it you lying in the morgue. She was still sitting there when Bridget came in. Guard Donlon told us the news, do you think, it's John I hope it is, at least we'll be able to give him a Christian burial. Bridget, Bridget please Grace said, please don't, do you think you could make me a cup of tea. You don't look too well Grace, will I fill you out a brandy. No thanks Bridget the tea will do just fine. Bridget sat at the table with Grace, she was talking about John, and what he had said and done during the summer, and wasn't it a pity what happened to him but now that his body was found, it will bring things to an end. Grace sat there, not really listening, her thoughts were on the task that she had to perform in the morning and she wasn't really sure if she could do it.

Grace arrived at the morgue at around ten o clock the guard got out and opened the car door. They went in together to a small waiting room. The Guard said wait here a minute I'll see if they are ready, he was back in a matter of minutes you can come in now he said. Grace stepped into the room. She saw a table with a body on it covered with a white sheet, a man was standing at the table, the guard but his hand on Grace's shoulder and brought her towards the table, she stood there looking down at the sheet. As the man lifted the sheet Grace closed her eyes, she heard the Guard say do you know him. Grace opened her eyes and looked.

No, no she said, with recognisable relief in her voice. The man at the table covered the body again, the Guard brought Grace back to the waiting room, they were some chairs there, she said to the Guard do you mind if I sit down. No not at all the Guard said take your time, I'll wait outside. Grace sat down and said to herself, Thank God it's not John, It's not John, she remembered Bridget saying something about that if it was John's body, it would bring it all to an end.

But Grace didn't want it brought to an end, somewhere deep inside she had hope, no matter how futile it was that Taigh was right and John was still alive, and that hope was all she had to keep her going, she remembered the words Taigh had said, gone but not dead, he is somewhere in the land of the living, Grace got up and walked out to the Garda car.

When Grace arrived home the threshing was in full swing, she changed and joined Bridget in the kitchen. Kathleen Casey had come up to help with the cooking. Bridget asked was the body John's. No Grace said. We still have hope then Kathleen said. We have Grace said, we have.

Bridget and Kathleen set the table in the kitchen, and brought another table from the parlour and set that as well so that all the men at the threshing could eat together. Some families in the parish had the disgusting habit of segregating the farmers from the workers at dinner time, but not in Grace's house, in this house all were equal.

The men came in at one o' clock, potatoes boiled in their skin, cabbage, and slices of hot bacon were served, jug's of milk were on the table to wash it down and several teapots of tea, when dinner was over several men stayed at the table smoking and talking, the talk was mostly about John and how he was missed, and how misfortunate Charles was to have lost his leg. At two o' clock the threshing machine started up again, Patsy and Paddy took up their position on the thresher, cutting bundles and feeding the thresher, Billy was on the straw rick to see that it was built properly, and for the rest of the day, tractor, thresher, and the men all worked as one.

It was thirsty dirty work, at four o' clock Grace and Bridget brought out bottles of stout for all the men, it was gratefully received and slugged down, some of the men who came from the neighbouring farms to help, had to return to those farms at five o' clock to milk the cows. At half six the thresher fell silent and the day's work ended.

Grace, Bridget and Kathleen had their supper together, the talk was of the days threshing, and of course John Grey. Kathleen said that it was as if, it was only yesterday when he came into her that Saturday in April, and she wiped the blood of his face. Bridget spoke of the day they went to the cove together and she went swimming in her underwear. Grace said, and I chastised you when you came back. God above she said it's hard to believe he's gone. They cleared the table, washed and dried the cups and dishes together. Then Grace walked out the lane with Bridget and Kathleen, and said Good night to them.

On the way back she walked through the haggard and stood looking at the thresher. John she said, John, what would you have thought of all this, what questions would you have asked, an Owl answered her from high up in an oak tree, the same tree that John had used for his analogy on the God's the first time he met father Richard, she crossed the yard to her door, the few remaining leaves on the trees whispered in the strong Autumn breeze, they seemed to say, in the land of the living, in the land of the living, in the land of the living, with that sound in her ears Grace closed the door behind her.

They resumed threshing again at eight the following morning, at three in the afternoon it was all over for another year, Grace stood and watched the tractor and thresher go out the lane, on its way to a neighbouring farm, and wondered will I ever again see a thresher. I am leaving the farm and valley where once I was so happy, but now with John gone there is nothing here for me only memories, but memories I can take with me, a line from the poem John wrote came to her mind. Tomorrow and forever I will think of you. I will John, I will.

Departure

The day after the threshing Bridget was in the yard washing churns, when Fr, Richard drove in the yard, hello Bridget he said, how are you, I'm fine she answered. Is Grace inside he asked. She's in the kitchen Father. Fr Richard entered the kitchen. Grace said hello and asked will you have some tea, Bridget and I have just finished, there's still some in the pot. I will thanks. Grace and Richard sat at the table, Richard placed a folder in front of Grace saying some papers in there for you to sign, we have a private offer on the farm it's more than we expected, our solicitor say we should accept. Grace Fr Richard said before you sign, will you consider, I was talking to Charles last night, he is very sorry for what happened and if you are willing to try and forget. Forget, forget, Grace said, how could I ever forget that he tried to rape Bridget here in this house and then tried to shoot John.

But surely Grace a second chance, he is a changed man. Can you be sure of that Richard, I gave him a second chance after he beat me on my wedding night, the fact is Richard we should never have married mistakes were made by you, your Father, my Father and me. When you recognise something as a mistake there is two ways you can deal with it, you can live with it, or you can walk away from it, and get on with the rest of your life, that's what I'm going to do.

But Grace Fr Richard said we all knew it would take time, we all knew at the start that you and Charles would have to get used to each other. Was I supposed to get used to the beatings as well. What about John Grey Grace, did he have anything to do with this. The only person that had nothing to do with mess is John Grey, this is entirely of our own making, if you and your father had accepted the woman that Charles was with, if he was brave enough to stand up to you both, I never would have met him, and when I did meet Charles if I hadn't made the selfish decision I made this would never have happened, so let's not blame anyone but ourselves, John Grey is not the cause of this.

But one thing I can tell you, if John Grey had come to the valley before I met Charles, this would never have happened now Richard let me see those papers, when she was satisfied with everything she signed. When does the new owner want to move in. As soon as possible Richard answered. I can be ready to go by Friday. You don't have to go that soon.

I want to Grace said, will you come out and bring me to the station. Of course Richard said, he took an envelope from his pocket, this is for Bridget it's from my Father and me, to say sorry for what happened. I'll see that she gets it Grace said, it will help give her a good start to married life she's made up her mind, she's going to marry Patsy. I must be going now Fr Richard said, I'll see you around ten on Friday, oh one more thing I spoke to the Bishop he has arranged an interview for you with a firm in Dublin. Thanks Grace said see you on Friday.

Grace and Bridget spent the next few days choosing what Grace would bring with her some of the larger things would go into storage, to be sent on later when Grace got her own place, for now she was going to stay with a friend she knew in college. Do you really have to go Grace, Bridger asked. Yes I do Bridget I can't stay here too many memories bad and good. You really liked him, John I mean. Yes I did. Would you stay if he was still here. Bridget Grace said, please, please don't. I'm sorry Grace it's none of my business. Bridget it's, it's not that, I, I just can't talk about it.

Richard drove in the yard at around ten on Friday morning, Grace and Bridget came out carrying a large suitcase each. Fr Richard took them and put them in the car. Richard Grace said the new owner, do you think he might keep on Bridget, Patsy and Billy it will be hard for them to find work. I'll speak to him Fr Richard said, he's new at farming I'm sure he'll want experience farm hands. There's none more experienced than those three, they practically ran this place all summer.

Grace turned and said good bye to Bridget, Patsy and Billy came out from the cow house and shook hands with Grace, Grace went to sit in the car, then hesitated and looked across at the workshop and at the window in John's room, she hadn't been in there since John had gone. She walked across the yard and entered the workshop.

There was sawdust on the work table and floor, a piece of timber that John had been cutting was still in the vice grip, Grace went towards the stairs and climbed slowly, she stood in the doorway looking into John's room, the bed clothes were pulled casually over the pillow, two mugs unwashed, and a book on the table, the kettle was on the stove, and the ashes of John's last fire was still in the grate, she entered the room, walked to the press. She took out John's photo, and gazed at it, went to the table and picked up the piece of wood that John had carved, finished and polished now.

It was a female, and male figure, arms around each other, head resting on each other's shoulder, on the back of the female figure the letter G was carved, and on the male figure the letter J, Grace opened the book on the table, a piece of paper that John was using as a marker fell to the floor, Grace reached down and picked it up it was the piece of paper that John had wrote the short poem on, standing there in the room on her own she read the poem.

I sit here and peace is mine, my heart is happy and so contented,
just to sit,   to dream, to be happy, all I ask is to be with you

forever / to cherish and to love you, and you to love me, to hold your hand, to share my life with you, to leave you never.

I must leave here and all this happiness will stay, but I will take with me a memory of you, and of this happy time, of your smile, you face / tomorrow and forever I will think of you, and remember how we laughed and loved in this time and place.

All things are planned for us, we plan nothing for ourselves.

Then an uncontrollable sob came from deep inside her followed by another, and another and all the sadness, loneliness and helplessness inside her burst forth in a torrent of tears. Bridget who had come up stairs was standing at the door she ran to Grace, and they stood there arms around each other. I miss him so, so much Grace said, no one knew, I couldn't tell anyone, I had to keep it all to myself until now. Let it out Bridget said, let it out, you'll feel better for it, they stood there for several minutes, Grace crying, Bridget consoling her. Then Grace took out a hanky and dried her eyes, put the photo, poem, and the little sculpture in her bag. I'm alright she said to Bridget, we better go down. Fr Richard will be waiting. Grace took a last look at the room where she had spent so many happy hours then walked down the stairs and closed the workshop door behind her.

Crossing the yard Bridget said you'll come back for the wedding. Thanks Grace said, I hope you and Patsy are very happy, but I won't be back, it's too soon, I couldn't, I don't know if I'll ever be back in the valley again, good bye Bridget and thanks for everything. Fr Richard drove slowly out of the yard, past the hayfield where the grass was now green again, along by the cornfield, now empty and bare except for some Crows foraging for seed, up the hill and over the brow, and Grace Arscott was gone from the valley of knockmurrin.

Discharged

At the same time that John Grey had vanished in the waters of Kilmurrin Cove, Mickell Power was opening his eyes and coming out of a coma at Waterford Regional Hospital, a nurse who was checking her chart noticed and immediately called a Doctor, the Doctor went to Mickell's bed and examined him, where, where am I he asked.

You're in Hospital the Doctor answered, and welcome back. In hospital Mickell said, why, why am I hear what's wrong with me, and what do you mean welcome back, where have I been. You tell us the Doctor answered, can you remember what happened, Mickell tried to sit up. Too soon for that, the Doctor said. I was up at Paddy Casey's, I left Paddy's to go home, walking down the hill I heard a tractor in the field, I climbed up on the fence to get a better view, I remember falling and that's it, what day is it Doctor. It's Saturday. Then I've just been brought in. You fell the Doctor said and hit your head. Mickell put his hand to his head. I can't feel anything he said. Oh that's long gone the doctor answered. What do you mean Mickell said.

The Doctor sat down beside the bed, Mr Power I have something to tell you. Am I all right Doctor. You're fine, considering what you have been through. Mr Power today is Saturday, but it's not the Saturday you fell. You mean I have been here for a week. We are now into September, you fell last April. What Mickell said, I've been here all summer, but surely that's not possible. It's possible all right, you did have us all worried, but now I think everything will be all right, we'll do a scan on Monday and some more tests, you will have to see the Physio, we have to get your muscles strong and active again, and if everything is alright we will send you home, the nurse have phoned your Parent's to tell them the good news, they are overjoyed and on their way in.

Two weeks later Mickell was ready to go home the Doctor was telling him all his tests were good, how, do you feel yourself. I'm grand Doctor, I just want to go home and make up for lost time. You can't go to work just yet, maybe in a week or so, in the mean time, plenty of walking, and maybe some bike work get those muscles back to normal, and I'll see you on Monday week. Doctor there's just one thing, I don't know if it means anything.

Tell me Mickel and I'll be the judge of that. I, I'm getting this vision, it flashes across my mind for a few seconds and then it's gone. That's strange the Doctor said, your scan was positive, all your tests are perfect, what kind of vision. It's of a young woman standing in a field of corn, and a reaper and binder in the field. A reaper and binder Mickel, you're way back in the years there. We will never fully understand the mind, you were in a coma for nearly six months, we know your mind was active during that time with eye movement and facial expressions, but we have no idea what was going on in there, or where your mind travelled to, what dreams or visions you had, several things must have gone through you mind over the last six months, this vision of the young woman you're having, was probably more dominant than the rest, and in your unconscious state was important to you, and it is still there, I'm sure it will fade with time, give it a few weeks, I'm sure by the time you come in for your check up it will have faded, now off you go, and don't worry.

Recognition

Mickell was home a week now and everything was going well, though he was still having the vision of the young woman in the corn field, taking the Doctor's advice he was walking to Kilmurrin cove for exercise. A black car was parked in the car park, he looked down the beach, a woman was standing at the water edge looking out to sea, a jacket hung loose over her shoulders, a few yards to her right another woman was taking photographs. Mickell assumed they were the owners of the car. He read the inscription on the memorial stone to the founder of the Kilmurrin Christmas day swim, a swim that had raised over half a million euro for various organisations in the City and County since its inception in nineteen eighty three.

He turned to walk home, then changed his mind and walked down the concrete path on to the sand and across the beach to the far side to the river, he saluted the woman who was taking photos, then walked back, he stood behind the woman who was looking out to sea and said, isn't this a wondrous wild place. His words seemed to have some effect on the woman, she just managed to keep her jacket from falling, then turned slowly around, she looked straight into Mickell's face, put her hand to her mouth to stifle a gasp. John, John Grey, you're John Grey she said in a low voice.

Mickell said no Mam, my name is Mickell Power. I, I'm sorry the woman said I mistook you for someone else, what you said about this place, what you called it, I have often heard it described like that. It is the only way to describe this place Mickell said. The woman reached out her hand, allow me to introduce myself, my name is Hannah Arscott-Lynch. Nice to meet you Mickell answered, then he said, Arscott, Arscott, I'm sure I've heard that name before, yes he said now I remember Paddy Casey mentioned a Grace and Charles Arscott, it's rather vague, the day I had my accident I'm sure he said they lived here in the valley, are you any relation. Yes, yes the woman answered Grace Arscott is my Mother, did you know her. No I'm afraid not that was long before my time.

Yes of course it would be, what was I thinking about, you are from the valley though, you know who you are. Why wouldn't I know who I am, I was bred born and reared here, but I don't know much about your Mother, Paddy promised to tell me the full story, but I didn't get a chance to get back to him.

Then a voice behind them said Mother are you all right. I'm fine she answered. Mickell turned around and was looking at a beautiful girl about the same age as himself. Then Hannah Arscott- lynch said, meet my daughter Grace. As he shook hands with Grace a clear vision of the woman in the cornfield flashed across his mind, and she was the image of the woman he was shaking hands with. Mickell put his other hand to his head.

Are you alright Grace asked. I'm fine Mickell answered, I had an accident, I fell and hit my head, I'm well again now, I get this vision of a woman standing, smiling at me in a corn field, with a piece of straw in her hair and I know you won't believe this, the girl in my vision is you,

Mickell was still holding the woman's hand. She said smiling. If you don't mind can I have my hand back. What Mickell said, then leaving her hand go he said I'm sorry. Hannah said you mentioned an accident. Yes Mickell said last April I fell and hit my head. I was in a coma. Hannah asked, when did you come out of the coma. I was in a coma from April to September. Hannah said did you ever hear of a John Grey. That's the person you mistook me for, the day of my accident Paddy mentioned him.

Many years ago Hannah said John Grey mysteriously came to this valley one Saturday in April, and vanished out of it in September. Mickell answered I suppose you could say John Grey was here in the valley for the duration that I was out of it. You could say that Hannah answered, that's a cold breeze in of the sea I think we should go to the car. Walking across the sand Hannah said, and since you came out of the coma you have a vision of a woman, and that woman is Grace.

Yes Mickell said, as clear as could be, in a cornfield, a lovely smile on her face, I can't explain it, turning to Grace he said believe me, the woman in my vision is you. I believe you she answered. Hannah said those who knew my Mother when she was Grace's age, say they are the image of each other, if you knew my Mother, you could have a picture of her in your mind and mistake her for Grace, but you just said you didn't know her, so where is the vision of Grace coming from.

Then she asked how is Paddy Casey my Mother often talks of him, is the Forge still there. No it's long gone, your Mother is she, how is she. She's not too bad a bit of dementia I had to come to Waterford on business, Charles Arscott died.   Her husband Mickell said. Yes Hannah answered, though they have been separated for years they never divorced, I never met him, when my Mother left this valley in fifty six she never returned, I was born in fifty seven in Dublin. Grace wanted to visit Waterford, so she came with me my husband is looking after Mother. In her mind now she spends a lot of time here in this valley.

When they reached the car Hannah said can we drop you anywhere, no thanks I need the exercise. Grace said, stand close to the memorial stone and I'll take your photo. Hannah said, make sure you don't show it to your Grandmother. Why Grace asked. I'll tell you later, then she said to Mickell would you mind if I gave you my phone number, I'd love to meet Paddy Casey, and find out more about John Grey, maybe you could arrange it. I'd love to Mickell answered, I'm sure Paddy would be delighted to meet you and your daughter, and maybe I might get to know more about the girl in my vision, and hope she might want to know more about me. Grace said, I am rather curious to know how I became the girl in your vision. Hannah and Grace sat in to the car. Hannah said bye for now, Grace said looking forward to meeting you again.

Hannah told Grace to stop the car at the top of Kilmurrin, Grace stopped at the exact spot that John Grey had stopped the pony and trap the day he and Grace were on their way back from Annestown, Hannah got out, and looked down into the valley at the lone figure walking up the road and said, John Grey, how, where did you come from, for she had no doubt from the moment she had looked into his face that Mickell Power and John Grey were the same person, she recognised him from the photograph she had got enlarged and framed for her Mother, and which had pride of place in her sitting room, Hannah had the original in her handbag, she couldn't understand it, couldn't explain, how someone who was the same age as her mother was over fifty years ago, could now be the same age as her granddaughter.

She tried to remember something about time, that her Mother used to say, something that John Grey had said, something about the past, the present, and the future, all she could remember was the end of it, is it yesterday, today, or tomorrow, were we here before, are we here now, will we be here again, she thought is that possible, could someone be here before, could they come back again, how in the name of God could someone look the same as they looked over fifty years ago, no, no she said, that could not happen, that made no sense.

And yet she was looking at a person walking up the road that proved it did make sense. What would she tell her Mother, that she had met John Grey, that he was about twenty three years old, no she couldn't tell her that, how could she, her Mother had never forgotten John Grey, how could he come back into her life now, how would she react, God she was confused enough, what would this it do to her, it was too late, all too late. Grace got out of the car are you all right Mother. I'm fine.

Grace looked at the figure on the road below and said it is strange he has in his mind a picture of someone he never saw. That would be strange Hannah answered, but maybe not so strange if it's a picture of someone he did see, but can't remember. I don't understand Mother. Neither do I Grace, neither do I. But if he didn't see you in the past, the way he looked at you on the beach I have no doubt he will see you in the future. They got back in the car and continued their journey to Waterford, Hannah rummaged in her hand bag, took out the photo of John Grey and the little sculpture that he had carved, it was wrapped in the poem he had wrote.

She said to Grace, when your Grandmother was first effected with dementia, she gave me these for safe keeping, she said to Grace have a look at this photo. Grace took it, and said that's, that's the man we just met, how, where did you get it. I got it from your Grandmother. Grace said I don't understand, where would she have got it from, she left here nearly fifty years ago and has never been back, how could she have a photo of someone who wasn't even born then.

I have no idea Grace it's a complete mystery to me, but until we can figure it out, I think it would be for the best not to show her the photo you just took of Mickell Power, all I can tell you is your Grandmother has treasured that photo and this little sculptor and poem all her life, if she should see the photo you have just taken how would she react, you take these Grace, and I hope they will bring to you the love they once brought to your Grandmother, she read the end of the poem, tomorrow and forever I will think of you, and remember how we laughed and loved in this time and place, all things are planned for us, we plan nothing for ourselves.

The End, or is it, the Beginning.